A Shortage of Angels

A Novel

A Shortage of Angels

A Novel

Penny Pickle

ROUNDFIRE
BOOKS

Winchester, UK
Washington, USA

JOHN HUNT PUBLISHING

First published by Roundfire Books, 2022
Roundfire Books is an imprint of John Hunt Publishing Ltd., No. 3 East St., Alresford,
Hampshire SO24 9EE, UK
office@jhpbooks.com
www.johnhuntpublishing.com
www.roundfire-books.com

For distributor details and how to order please visit the 'Ordering' section on our website.

ISBN: 978 1 80341 374 7
978 1 80341 375 4 (ebook)
Library of Congress Control Number: 2022915386

A CIP catalogue record for this book is available from the British Library.

Design: Lapiz Digital

◆

UK: Printed and bound by CPI Group (UK) Ltd, Croydon, CR0 4YY
Printed in North America by CPI GPS partners

We operate a distinctive and ethical publishing philosophy in
all areas of our business, from our global network of authors to
production and worldwide distribution.

Contents

All things work together for good for those that love the Lord.
Romans 8:28

For Peter and Neely

Prologue

I have heard many folks laying out their errant incantations of the Judgment Day. And any time I hear someone declaring the Judgment to be from God on mortal beings, I know that the orator has no business talking.

Oh sure, there will be a reckoning and a revelation. In the hereafter for each arriving soul, revelation is the unveiling of the life's mission. It is the day when it is self-revealed, whether or not the soul fulfilled its assignment, or to what degree our dreams came to fruition. The judgment is not from God on us. We execute these judgments upon ourselves.

We are faced with accepting and relishing our outcomes, or orchestrating the completion of these purposes in eternity, when the soul is no longer in bodily form.

Indeed, it would be our fervent desire for the Great White Throne Judgment to be imposed by God. Because God is forgiving.

—Rev. C. J. Ellison, Tent Revivalist

My name is Calvinia Jean Prather and I can tell you right now, I've got a gift.

But before you think I'm talking about myself too fancy and proud, this gift was something I didn't conjure up or beckon to myself. So, I am not claiming this in a bragging, smart-alecky way. It was a secret at first, even to me.

The gift hid itself, maybe waiting until I cleared my mind of things that don't really matter. Setting up housekeeping in the back of my head, it came out from time to time in little pieces. I couldn't always put my finger on it. But I knew it wasn't right to be in a hallway all by myself, and then feel somebody brush me from behind. To top it off, it didn't scare me when it happened. It was lightly peculiar in the beginning, so I didn't even give it the time of day.

When I went into a spell from my gift, I was transported to the depths of my soul, during sacred moments when I could commit my mind fully. I was usually dizzy-headed and felt like I was dreaming, or watching a movie of myself. Sometimes I walked into a room and knew for sure somebody was there by the feeling in my bones, or I thought maybe somebody behind me was reaching through the window. Each time I looked for them, I felt a heavy stillness so quiet, I could hear my shoes crease as I stepped. When I checked the windows and doors they were latched shut.

Sometimes I pitched back, caught with a glare that blinded both eyes so bad that I thought my number was up. But no, it was not my time.

In my younger days, I was accused of putting bobby pins in electric sockets. And I have to say, guilty as charged. There always followed, a long pantomimed scolding about what it would be like to get electrocuted. But when I did it, I never felt anything but the swirl of a cool flying breeze. Many are the folks who have felt the passing draft. Few are those who can see the angels who created the cool gust. But I can see, because that is my gift.

1

The Gift

Most people don't cotton to the idea that there are angels everywhere around us. But I can tell you honestly, first hand, that there are. Because I got it straight from Clovis Ray Palmer Jr., premature baby, dead as a doornail on arrival.

It all started innocently and reverently. I was simply paying my respects to the dearly departed. Clovis Ray was lying in the parlor of his mama and daddy's house on a buffet table draped with doilies and lace. He never drew a breath of air and was no more than two hours old.

I had the privilege of meeting him because my granddaddy, Packy, who I live with since I've got no mama, is a mortician. And we were right in the middle of supper when we had to 'up and take a baby casket to the Palmer's. The casket was carved from the finest mahogany with black cherry stain.

Baby caskets are made of nicer wood because they are smaller, but they cost the same as big ones. Families just aren't happy if they don't pay a right smart amount when a baby dies. I guess they want to be fair, since they get out of paying for college.

When we pulled through the Palmer's gates on their grand circular drive, Packy ordered me to stay in the car in his medium voice. Though I am not prone to outright disobedience, after a while I had to pee so bad my eyeballs were starting to float. One more chill and I would have done something that I would never have done, especially not in the big black Cadillac that rides folks to Memory Land. I commenced to squirming like a worm on a fish hook.

Lord forgive me, I had to find me a powder room. So, I poured out of the Cadillac and slinked up the back steps. When

3

I slipped through the kitchen, I heard Packy comforting Tressie, the Palmer's maid, on the stairway. The parlor was the only place to duck into and that's where most people lay out their kinfolk. Sure 'nough, that's where I met Clovis Ray.

I would not enter a place where the departed was laying without paying my respects. I may only be a fifth grader at Mirabeau B. Lamar Elementary, and as Packy would say, in the year of our Lord nineteen hundred and sixty eight, but I've been taught my manners.

Oh, the room was grand alright. The rug was such thick fine wool that I felt two inches taller when I walked on it. You could bet the Palmers would be paying in cash. They owned ever' little porcelain-faced doll and poodle figurines you could ever imagine, along with the antique car decanter collection that Avon put out, all still full to the brim. The bottles made the parlor smell sweet against the musty, aging wood of the Duncan Phyfe Antiques. It was a cheap smell like bitter clove that would in time give you a headache.

Packy already spread him out for the first viewing, real pretty. He draped the lid with a satin baby blanket that Tara, our help, makes up for infant funerals. His of course, was baby blue.

At first, I thought a draft was blowing the baby blanket because it rustled a little. When I came closer, I felt somebody there. The urge to pee backed up all the way to my throat, and I do believe my heart quit beating.

I tiptoed over holding my petticoat so steady, I could have balanced myself on a high trapeze. I tried to chin up on the side of the buffet to see in the infant coffin. Then something mashed the top of my fingers and pressed the back of my head hard enough for my bangs to jump. I wasn't too scared since those things happened to me before.

I looked around the still room and then decided to hike up on a fancy stool I found with a needlepoint Chinese pug wearing a George Washington outfit. I stood beholding the poor little fellow.

Though a fine woman's hanky covered Clovis Ray's face, I saw big blue veins running ziggety-zaggety across his head, plumb through the cloth. Bless his heart; his mama had him in a white christening dress. *Good thing you didn't make it if your mama was going to sissify you like that*, I thought to myself.

I pulled up the tiny dress to see his round little belly. You could see deep into his skin like looking through white grapes that have seeds in them. I bet I could see to bone if I'd had a flashlight. His eyes were closed tight even though I knew Packy hadn't stitched them yet. His head had fuzz, not hair, just peach skin, golden with a hint of copper. All the bones in his chest stuck out, barrel shaped like a grandma smoker. His ears were melted to his head like a plastic baby doll you've put a match to, and they were set a might lower than you'd expect. He clutched a rattle with one hand and the tips of his fingers were shiny, but he had no fingernails to speak of.

His legs were curled up like pretzels, almost in a knot. I guess he would have been mighty limber if he had made it. Maybe he'd have been a prize limbo dancer. I put his little dress down and went to looking for a neck. His head was set flat on his shoulders. *Something ain't right about this baby*, I said to myself. *I bet his problem is genetical.* I was thinking hard on what his predicament might have been when I heard a throat being cleared. Then I felt somebody blow on the side of my face. Naturally I just froze, and thanked the good Lord for helping me to the ripe age of nine and a half. It would of course be my last year, when Packy got through with me. Horseplay and other shenanigans are fine and dandy at home, but business puts food on the table, and Packy has made clear the lines he draws for such matters. I was prepared to turn around and see my granddaddy patting his toe on the fancy wool rug. Then the baby blanket rustled again.

My sight was clouded on the sides like there was a vapor there, with coolness around it. I saw a soft white glow, and my blinking could not clear it.

"You don't have one mortal thought in your head, do you?"

That voice was not Packy.

I turned my head to the right and I was almost seeing double. There was a kid perched up on the closed end of the coffin. But this kid had a neck and fingernails, and a head of hair. Though he favored the dead infant, the cauliflower ears were gone with normal ones set in their place.

"That's how come you can see me. That much I already know but I've got a lot more to learn. Yep. The seraphims came to get me and they were straightening my wings. Then there was some sort of dust up over in Africa. Seeing as I was just released, they said they would come back for me since I'm not a fast flyer yet. 'Go ahead and comfort your parents, they said, and we'll be back.'"

He looked upward and seemed in deep thought for a moment. "There's a shortage of angels you know."

"Uh, no I didn't know," I said sheepishly.

"That's right. To the point now where mostly we come to those that want us enough to call us, special purpose people and hardened hearts. Most can't see us like you can. It means you can take worldly clutter from your mind. You must be good at concentrating to the heart of things." He smiled as if I was owed a little bit of honor.

"Really," I said, puffing up like a rooster. I started thinking about how special or smart I must have been to see actual angels when Clovis Ray started to fade away. I was upset and mad at myself for trying to be so fancy. I closed my eyes up tight and looked hard at the backside of my eyelids until I could see nothing but squiggly lines and glitter balls. When I opened my eyes again, Clovis Ray returned like our Zenith does when it is interrupted by a jet flying overhead.

He smiled patiently at me and then he pulled his little wings around and smoothed his hands around their crests. Two medium-sized wings arched in the middle of his back, and two smaller round ones attached around about his sacrowheeliyak, where the spine meets the tailbone.

"Course I just have four wings now. Fact is I will just have four for about the next thousand years. Then I'll be a seraphim too," he announced in an accomplished fashion.

"You get new wings do you? I mean, in a thousand years?"

"No not a whole new set. You get to add your wings of light. Anybody knows you can't go in the highest sanctum bare-eyed."

"Goes without sayin' I guess." He was mighty interesting indeed, but sadly my body had not yet lost its concern for a powder room.

He looked at the puzzlement on my face and politely went on. "When you get your wings of light, you can go into the actual arena surrounding the throne of the Great I Am. But the light is mighty bright. It's so bright that you can't stand it. The seraphims have two extra wings at shoulder height to shield their eyes from the magnificence. Sometimes they lie at the foot of the throne all day just to praise and worship." Clovis Ray had put his hands over his eyes to show me and was swinging his boney legs with real excitement.

"The lights are too bright, you say? Are you up there with the sun?"

Clovis Ray paused and pulled his hands off of his face. He gave off a little pestered huff and shook his head. "No, the Great I Am is the light, and brighter than the sun. That is where we receive our illumination. You know, that's why we glow."

He held his arms out straight in front of him and looked at them up and down and side to side. "See I just barely have a low white light now. I'm just starting out. I'll see what my true color is over time."

Clovis Ray reared back and spread his wings and tried to move down to the floor. He went a might faster than he expected, hit ground and went to his knees. He was a little shy after that, and took a deep breath and surveyed his arms again.

"I want my true color to be blue. There aren't many blues you know. Blue is the hottest part of a flame." He made a fanning motion with his hands to emphasize the blue heat and gave me a toothy grin.

"When will you know?" I clenched my shoulders and tapped my foot in a clockish rhythm. I was trying to draw my body's focus away from my cantaloupe-sized bladder.

"Oh it will take years, depending on my works. I could be any color, anywhere from low white like this," he said side-eyeing his arms again, "to amber, or lavender. It depends on how much light I give off along my way. If I don't lose any light, I suppose I could be a bright fiery red like Lucifer." When he said that he chuckled to himself a little.

"Lucifer!" I said with a shudder. I had to squeeze my legs together even harder so as not to pee my pants, and switched myself around. My body got so heated up, the Mexican jumping beans started clicking in my pocket.

Clovis Ray made a shushing sound and put his palm out to hush me. "Yes, Lucifer."

He took a moment to form his words and was more serious. "There is a master plan. And we have to abide by that plan. The world works itself out." He turned his palms up and shrugged. He picked up a mirror and looked at himself from ear to ear, and then sat it down.

"We are just on standby to guide and comfort through man's own decisions. But sometimes we get too involved and we angels try to intervene with what powers we do have. And when we do, our light begins to fade, and we get weighed down. But Lucifer? No one ever asks him to do anything good because they forget that he is an angel. So, his light has built up for so long that he is like a million red coals of fire when he passes by."

Clovis Ray was an earnest little fellow for sure, and I believed him to be telling me the truth. I don't think he was name dropping Lucifer to impress me. But if it is just a story, he can sure spin a decent yarn.

He let his shoulders drop and let out a sigh. "Yeah, old Lucifer, he is the morning star, the light bearer. He let his pride get in the way. It was kind of like, you know, he wanted to start his own business. He thinks if he could get all the angels on his side, he would control the light and take the Great I Am's power." Clovis shook his head and looked down before he looked back at me. "You know he is the only angel that can't go into the high sanctum?"

He rubbed his chin and then shrugged his shoulders. "But he is still an angel, and he'll take any light he can get."

Clovis Ray smiled a little smile and nodded as though he'd said something deep and fluttered his little wings so that he lifted himself up over the table, then he crossed his legs to sit back down. He reached over his shoulder where his wings of light should be and beamed with a longing smile.

"And you'll get your wings of light in a thousand years?" I asked as though I was congratulating him on an upcoming event.

"If I don't take another tour." He made a tsk sound and slowly licked his lips.

Clovis stopped talking for a minute and closed his eyes. He squinted hard and brightened his light. When he moved his arms and legs a blur of light followed them.

"Oh yeah." He went on. "We sink when we intercept prayers, or act on things we see playing out. We can sink all the way to the earth's core where we have to be born all over again. But it is hard when you have love and sympathy for people."

"Seems like you could have lived a while."

"See now, there you go, that right there." He shook his little pointer finger at me. "That's how angels get caught up and start sinking. This is the Great I Am's plan and no one must interfere." He lowered his head and thought for a moment. "But if my mama had cried out to the angels to save me, things could have been different." Clovis Ray embraced a happy picture of his parents and kissed them before he put it back down. "Or my parents could have gotten the message without this short assignment."

Clovis Ray finished that statement with closed eyes and an affirming nod, like a little preacher. But looking back up to me, he seemed embarrassed and peered off to one side. He looked like a kid that had just broken a vase or something and then heard his mama coming down the hall. I thought to pick him up and comfort him for a moment. Despite his smart talking, he was by time standards, just a baby.

Then I got my dizzy spell, and my vision blurred a little. Things looked the way they do on the television when someone starts to dream and the whole screen stirs up like pond water. In the clearing haze, three bodies of light loomed over Clovis Ray's head. One angel was lavender and the other two were different shades of pink. The visions formed into grand women with wings lightly fluttering away the haze. My eyes began to focus as fresh coolness flushed my cheeks. Images of the heavenly beings were coming together, and I could see majestic and powerful wings holding them up with two small wings coming up from behind their necks that had a hand-like look about them. It was as if they were fans made from crossing graceful swan necks and the hands of fairy princesses. They wore flowing robes that draped down until they turned to swirling smoke.

I could not read the angels' faces, to know if they would be kind to me or ignore me. I was desperate to communicate with them and meet them as I did Clovis Ray. But their faces were like stone, not frowning but not smiling either. Behind their eyes I sensed the quiet wisdom of a thousand years. Serenity filled my heart like pouring cool water in a desert well and it soothed every bone in my body. I stood so content, I wouldn't have left for the powder room if the room caught fire.

"The special purpose child can see you, Asmin." The lavender one in the middle said to Clovis Ray. Purple infused her with an eminence the color of Jesus' robe in Church paintings and lilac streams of light took the place of her hair. She had no pupils in her eyes, just crescents of violet with passing clouds inside them.

Clovis Ray, came closer to her feet and tipped his head as if that was his name all along. He bowed his head silently and waited.

"The child can see us as well, Maraeze." This time the magenta angel on the right spoke. Her voice was deep and throaty. Her light was round and twinkling and her face was like a moon. Her position was just a smidge lower than the other angels and she had to flap her wings rapidly from time to time to stay afloat. The light pink angel on the left fluttered back a bit like she was bowing away and little wisps of clouds swam into her wake. They stationed themselves in the air and eyeballed me for a minute.

"Can you accept this charge, child?" Maraeze asked. "A special purpose child who can bring her mind to the clarity of seeing heavenly beings has a mighty charge."

"I..." The coolness had dried and cracked the back of my throat and my words wouldn't come out. "I don't understand," I managed to choke out.

"If you want to remain a child who can play and do childish things, we can remove this memory from you, my sweet. You may continue your life as always. But if you choose to continue as a special purpose child, you may be called upon to intervene in earthly things, and see us now and again, as we go about our work. You will have responsibilities not usually borne by children. Shall I wipe this moment from your mind?"

"No!" I said after I swallowed hard and found my voice. "I want to see you."

"As you wish," she said with a bow of her head. "We must not tarry but remember this. There is fear and there is love, only these two things. Love will fulfill you; fear will grip you and you will feel the negative energy. Release it and exchange it for an action of love and you will be protected. In all things, act in love as the Great I Am acts in love, and this will accomplish your missions." She waited for a moment and sized me up again. "You will know you have made a wrong decision when you do not feel at peace. This is your measure."

"Yes, ma'am," I said with respect.

"Where is your guardian, child?" Maraeze asked.

"My what, ma'am?" I bowed a little more humble, not wanting to look stupid.

"Her guardian?" She looked at the quiet, light pink angel.

"Evangelise," she answered softly.

The light pink one and I both bowed so low and reverent that one of us was about to end up on the floor. Her movements were graceful and ceremonial.

"Evangelise!" Maraeze called. The voice echoed like mine when I holler in our well house.

I felt more coolness and my bangs were blown flat on my head as a glittery light pierced the room from above the fireplace. It was a topaz light with amber edges and gold. Evangelise was the most beautiful angel yet.

"This child's ability to see us; is it according to the master plan, Evangelise?" Maraeze asked her.

"Yes," Evangelise answered.

"Not of your accord?"

"No, Maraeze. I have not revealed myself before to this child." Evangelise answered. There was something like twilight in her voice. It was a little twangy, but soft, with southern calm. I wondered if this angel ever spoke to me in my sleep.

"Very well then, child," Maraeze said to me.

I did not hear Maraeze for a moment because I was taken with Evangelise. I felt as if she could wash away any wrong I had ever done. Her light glowed so that it almost had a sound.

Maraeze waited dryly until I snapped back to attention. My face flushed red when I realized I was holding everybody up. "Use your gift only for the higher good. Live in faith and know that things, though they may not appear so, are unfolding as they should. Any attempt to intercede will only interfere with the plan of the Great I Am."

"The plan, ma'am?" I said.

She turned to Clovis Ray but didn't speak to him. She turned back to me and spoke like a teacher. "I think Asmin may have spoken to you of it. The plan is for the healing of the earth and humankind. This endeavor we must all support with our very being, and never stray from our purpose towards this end, be we human or celestial. We are not to intervene in earthly matters unless directed. We are only to support and cherish humanity as destinies unfold."

"Yes, ma'am," I said obediently.

"Evangelise?" she said looking at my angel.

"So it is," Evangelise answered and bowed.

Maraeze nodded as if telling them all it was time to move onward. Evangelise and the pink angel departed. The magenta one jump-started herself to take wing, her body seeming heavier than the rest. Maraeze turned back to me.

"Remember, though you know of us, you cannot ask us to lose our height and light over you," she said soundly. With that she turned to Clovis Ray.

"The Garden of Prayer, Asmin," Maraeze directed.

"Yes," he said as she disappeared. He gave me a loving look and turned to depart after her. A gush of purple light and flame encircled him and lifted him up.

But I couldn't just let him go off. "Clovis," I said. He kept on. "Clovis Ray!" I said a little louder. He turned, hovering over me but said nothing. "How do I see you again?" I asked him.

"Think loving thoughts," he said, "like heaven."

***

I was jolted out of my trance when Tressie threw her hands up to her cheeks and gasped that I was all the way up on the buffet with Clovis Ray. She literally scared the pee out of me and I nearly washed the pug stool out from under me like somebody let go a dam.

Thank the good Lord, Tressie was a sight more interested in cleaning up that puddle and the pug stool than telling it on me. I ran out in the backyard and rinsed myself off with the water hose. I threw my soaked panties behind the Palmer's holly bushes, far back as I could throw them without getting pricked. I held my dress down tight and trotted back to the car.

When Packy loaded the little coffin into the silver braces, all closed up with Clovis Ray inside, I didn't want to talk. I just wanted to remember my visit with Clovis Ray and the angels as long as I could. I played possum in the front seat and since he thought I was asleep, he drove us home in quiet.

2

Onward

Oh, the irony that we are given eyes to see. They are captured by the physical world with such an onslaught of scenes and happenings, the busyness of which blinds us from visualizing the spiritual. We amble around day-by-day in search of clues for instant pathways to success in the material, while all true treasures are held on the other side of the great partition. We believe that Jonah was swallowed by a whale, a storybook fable and impossible event to survive. We choose this rather than "seeing" that this was in actuality a period of great spiritual introspection before being regurgitated back to the physical with new insights of inner prosperity and satisfaction. Subsequently Jonah, could be robbed of material goods, it is true, ad infinitum. But none could touch or steal the wealth of joy that multiplied within him.
—Rev. C. J. Ellison, Tent Revivalist

I felt proud when I thought back on Packy, coming down the Palmer's steps with that little coffin. He was so gentlemanly and kind with dead folks that I learned how to act by him. He taught me respect by the kind of man he was. My granddaddy could soothe the most hysterical families into a calm reverence when they followed suit with him. His honor and adoration for the human spirit provided a healing salve on people's sore hearts and his words pacified the loved ones who were left behind.

I was pleased to say Packy was a handsome man, and not just because he was my granddaddy. He was tall and thin like Abraham Lincoln, and I don't figure anyone around our parts could whip him. The hair on his face was more salt than pepper and was trimmed to a thin line down his cheek with no moustache. He had a dent in his chin and a scar where he was hit with the tongue of a cotton trailer, but it was neatly covered. His eyes were gray and his lips were pursed tightly, never wavering to tell the truth.

He had eight charcoal gray suits that were sported everywhere he went, in case he got a call. Only the color of his neckties changed against his crisp white cotton shirts with pen markings leading into the pocket. Neatly shined black cowboy boots adorned his feet, and were worn until his sock showed through and then he had new soles put on them. His legs were long, with nothing but meat on his bones, and there wasn't much he needed a ladder to reach.

Friday morning was Packy's time to do his chores in town. We'd go early, and ever since I turned eight, he'd let me take off by myself. I liked to walk around and think, stretch my legs a bit. It didn't matter if he beat me to the car because he was happy passing the time, talking somebody's ear off. He'd get the men all riled up and they'd talk about the unfair this and common-sense-defying that. Almost any subject they picked had something about gettin' cheated in it. When they finished, they felt they were upstanding citizens and doing the best they could, against all odds and tainted circumstances. Goodbye was never said, when they went their separate ways. An affirming nod was the end of their meeting, as they prepared to go back to toiling against twists of fate and the hardships of their ever'day lives.

Onward was a somber little town. The town entry sign said "ONWARD Christian Soldiers," and smaller under it said, "A Town Full of God-fearing People."

The only thing I wanted to do was see the angels, but I was having a hard time quieting my mind. I decided to stop trying so hard and clear my thoughts by walking the streets of Onward to ruminate on other things.

As I strolled down Beech Street, I saw neglected houses, scarred and tattered like the people living inside them. Folks liked to keep themselves good and numb, either with liquor or countless quoting of the Bible, telling everybody what they wanted them to hear, and saying God said it.

I could look ahead and see the blurry heat radiating off the blacktop on Beech Street. The road edges shoved off in waves where the sun got so hot it made it soft and tires pushed up the street edges like pie crusts. Yards were filled with clumps of dallisgrass that shot up green and hardy like it was the only thing getting enough water to live in the hot Texas sun. Tiny hidden burr stickers pierced your foot the same, green or dry.

Honeysuckle vines were weighty and cumbersome over chain link fences as bees and hummingbirds stole their bounty. Each tiny trumpet I plucked had one small drop to sweeten my tongue for as long as I had the patience to pluck them.

I longed to pull a blossom from the many pampered magnolia trees with splattered roots along the street. One blossom floating in a bowl at my bedside would hold its fragrance in my room for a week, even long after the white wore to brown.

Like a fly to sugar, I was drawn to a lumbering water sprinkler, aimlessly fanning a parching yard. Its cool misty water reflected the sun so directly on me, that I saw a rainbow when I cocked my head a certain way. An aproned lady looked at me from her screen door, but said nothing. I figured I should move on my way.

The scorching street was better than the grassy shortcuts full of the chiggers, so I kept off from them. I didn't need Tara dotting me with her purple fingernail polish to choke off their oxygen and kill them. It was all over but the crying when I went to scratching. I do not understand why God makes things itch if scratching spreads it.

I passed many a yard that had cars parked up close to the front porch. People drove up so fool drunk they just fell out and rolled into the house. They sometimes kicked at the car door to shut it, but were seldom successful. They had the nerve to cuss each other and their children for the gaping doors the next morning when the car battery was dead, from the inside lights burning all night. Then they acted like "Why me, God? I'm already broke down," like God did it to them and they ain't responsible.

I liked to pick myself up some colored glass that was lying along the road. It was mostly green and brown, occasionally blue from milk of magnesia bottles. The milkier the color, the longer I knew it had been lying around out there getting rubbed by the dirt and sand. I picked up a piece of red and felt maybe the day was lucky. Red might be the rarest glass of all. I peered through it as if it was magical, hoping to see angels through it, but nothing showed.

I kicked a can the length of four old lady houses. Without a doubt, I was going to hear organ music from their soap operas. Sure 'nough I heard the organist hold down a long high note which meant something happened that was shocking. Or maybe somebody came clean with a secret this or that, or they found out who the real father was. Usually happy chords were hit on a first kiss for what seemed to be an unlikely couple, after many episodes of working up to it. They sometimes switched to piano, soft and low if someone was missing out on love. The real cliffhangers always aired on Friday to keep everybody interested over the weekend.

Wind wafting through checkered curtains tainted the air with the smell of stale bacon grease saved up every morning from breakfast. It was a prime ingredient in everything they served, save drinking water.

Suddenly, I was caught with the aroma of fresh baking like Mrs. Applebaum's homemade apricot turnovers, that got my stomach to talking. Mrs. Applebaum even puts a touch of bacon grease in her crusts. If she sees me, she will call me from the window to come fill the delicate pastries with the soft, honeyed fruit and fork down the edges. An hour of labor will yield me one turnover that we will split together. And she won't let me do the splitting.

I see that Mr. Applebaum is out with a basket of fresh pastries for sale ahead of me. His shoulders shake right to left as he clomps down the street with one short leg. Since he is already selling, that means I won't get one today unless the trail of dogs clipping his heels finally tips him over.

Packy says some folks try to steer clear of the Applebaums, because they are Jews. Not me. I hold a little extra respect and humbleness towards them. I don't know if Jesus' last name is Applebaum or not 'cause the Bible doesn't tell you. But I know he is a Jew, and that means they have a lot better chance of being kin than I have.

I came upon Mr. Hubert's yard and heard him playing a piano piece fit for the Miss Texas pageant. His four o'clock bushes have grown tall and full, and their blossoms are closed. When the air begins to cool and the sun begins to fade, hot pink flowers will pop out everywhere with exploding color. He has planned his yard just so, where something is blooming all the time and it looks like a picture from a fairy tale book. There are elephant ears in the bright sun because they can take the heat, and spider lilies of orange and crimson are waving too. He coddles his geraniums and gardenias closer to the porch where he can keep them watered every day. It is rumored that he uses coffee grounds to make the soil more acid, and that is why he has the largest azalea beds in Onward.

I was not allowed to take piano lessons from Mr. Hubert, for reasons that were never clear. Once, I heard a neighbor tell Packy not to let me around Mr. Hubert because he was a Homo sapien and walked like one too. Packy said just because he wasn't married did not qualify him to be called that, and no one should make fun of a man's infirmities. I don't know what in tarnation marriage and funny walking has to do with it. My teacher, Miss Annie Mae, has never been married and she is the very one who taught us that we are Homo sapiens, one and all. And when she walks, she does it with sheepish tiny steps, holding a hankie to her chest in one hand while she straightens her skirt with the other. But if I had busted in and said "We are all Homo sapiens, I know it because I studied them in school," I might have had to take piano lessons. So for once, I kept my mouth shut.

My stomach beckoned me again and I reached inside my front pocket to see if I had change for Mr. Applebaum and his treats. I found nothing inside but a fraying hole. Dang the luck, as I kept walking on down the street, I saw Moody. I was smack dab in the middle of the block with no bushes or cover to hide in and no place to go but forward.

It ain't that I don't like Moody or have anything against retarded folk, but it seems to me that he has a few dim bulbs on his Christmas tree, and I didn't want him traipsing behind me. He was playing so hard at sword fighting with a Bois d'arc tree that he didn't even see me. You have to be touched in the head to fight with a Bois d'arc tree. That tree will eat you up. It has thorns like fishhooks. The more you get hung on them, the deeper they go, and the tree will draw you in like a giant suction cup. *Why isn't he fighting with the dogwood or the crepe myrtle tree?* I thought shaking my head.

Then I went to feeling bad. He was pitiful with his only friend, a tree. Least the tree wasn't making fun of him, and shaded him from the cruel sun. I said *Lord, I am sorry for calling Moody a retard even if it wasn't out loud.*

"Mornin', Moody," I said to him.

"Huduh," he said with wide-eyed astonishment. His words didn't come out right because of the slobber that bolted out his mouth and down his shirt. He went to smiling and blushed. Then he closed his eyes, looking down and tried to scratch his noggin. He forgot he had his play sword in his hand and whacked himself in the back of the head. That set off a chain reaction of spastic fits and he started throwing the sword around until I was afraid he was going to put his eye out. He would be black and blue before dinnertime if I didn't move on.

He straightened up like all was well and he had a grip on himself and tried not to appear affected. I smiled back a fake, cracky smile and tried to act like he was normal.

And the truth was he would have looked near normal if he would quit going off and cutting his own hair. It looked like a field of mesquite trees on top of his head. He was covered in pimples, and he picked on his face so he looked like a peanut rounder. He wore gray horn rims like a daddy would wear. His pants legs never ended up anywhere near his ankles and the backs of his socks always rode down into his shoes. And why did he wear a necktie every day of the week? I guess he was just attempting to throw off being different by looking smart. I couldn't figure out if the grease in his hair was Brylcreem or lack of hygiene. But I never caught wind of him stinking.

As I sashayed on by, Moody had just enough smarts to follow me, but not too close. He probably knew about rock-throwing distance and stayed outside that range. I casually placed my hands in my hip pockets and accidentally found myself a shiny fifty-cent piece. Too far past the Applebaum's my mouth filled with water when I thought about the sweet raspberry filling at the Dough-nut, next to the bank downtown.

But it was mighty hot by the time I rounded the corner of Beech and Pine, and I was glad to see the ice plant just ahead. Jelly donuts could wait a little minute while I cooled myself down a bit and regained my strength. I sneaked up the ramp through the back door until I could see the freshly frozen rectangles on the chopping bay. I laid down on a block of ice as big as my bed, long as I could stand it. I played like I was on a frozen planet that dropped off to nowhere on the other side of the plastic streamer curtains that hung in the doorways.

The Black men who were going back and forth from the loading area wouldn't say a word to me because I'm White. I don't know if that is because they don't like me for being White, but I doubt it, because when no one was looking they smiled at me. My life is better than theirs in some ways but in others it equaled out because I had to wear shoes all the time and they got to go barefoot. They got to wear clothes that were their favorites because they wore the same ones every day, and nobody made them throw them out when they got raggedy. There is nothing worse than stiff, new, scratchy clothes and dresses when it ain't a school day.

When I was about to need a doctor for frostbite, I moseyed on back outside and sure enough Moody was trying to hide behind a wood panel station wagon. He thought that when he covered his eyes, I couldn't see him, even with his body showing.

I stopped for a minute and went into that trance I go into sometimes, but it seemed stronger. All of a sudden, I felt as if I was the only real human around and everybody else was just part of a stage. The world around me flattened out like a picture painting on a giant canvass. I reckoned I had let my head get too cold on the ice or I froze off my blood from pumping.

Looking upward, by golly, there they were again. Finally. My stomach squeezed into one big ball and dampened the pangs of my hunger.

Angels were making their way over towards downtown and I knew that something was about to happen. They were solemn in their approach and reverent, flying slowly. I made better time running than a Shetland pony, leaving Moody behind with his hands clapped over his eyes.

Following the stream of their fading light was hard from street level because I was blocked by honking cars and Lyonel the hobo trying to stop me for a match. I finally could see freely when I reached the courthouse square with its broad streets and slow red lights. There was a school bus full of tennis players lined out the door at the Dough-nut, but I couldn't have cared less for a jelly donut anyway with angels around.

On the south corner, the angels' route stopped short as the bright yellow light never flowed past the roof of the Onward

National Bank. I was dead still and concentrated while surveying the area. Not much was going on around me except Brother Delaney, head deacon at the Baptist church, leaning against the brick wall. I thought he might get to verse-quoting at me, so I pictured myself invisible and hoped to get by him with my spy-walking quietness. The last thing I had time for at this exciting point was exploring my hereafter with a blowhard like H. L. Delaney.

Brother Delaney just loved for the preacher to go out of town because he got to be a lay minister and preach the sermon. Nobody left the church with their head up when Brother Delaney got off the podium, and the offering plate hit all-time highs. He was a spindly man, skinny and white knuckled because he thought he didn't deserve full helpings. That way he could stack up points for unselfish suffering and deny himself the simple joys that Jesus was not accustomed to having. He had his wife, Rosemary, cut his hair close to his head every Sunday night so he could tell anybody he saw with long hair that they needed a good haircut.

Rosemary was the church organist and she could wear an organ out. She loved to play the old Fanny J. Crosby hymns, but Brother Delaney wouldn't let her play them on his preaching Sundays because Crosby tunes went too light on sinners. He liked to hear "Are you washed in the Blood?" and "Alas and did my Savior bleed?" His favorite word was wretch.

To escape his witnessing, I tried to blend with the sidewalk, best I could, to make it to the last pad of concrete between Bro. Delaney and the building doors. Luckily, he got taken up with another sinner passing by, and I reached safety at the rotating glass doors of the bank. I pushed the handle all the way through without my usual ride around.

When I looked across the lobby, I noticed that Rosemary Delaney and their little girl named Caroline were boarding the elevator. Such a smart and proper-looking lady, Rosemary had her on a dupioni silk dress and it wasn't even Sunday. She had on skin-colored hose with not one snag, pumps and purse to match. I would not say that she was fat, just pleasingly plump and jolly looking. Her usual smile turned a little bit strained when she pulled Caroline past the gap between the elevator and the shaft.

Loading on the cage elevator was a little tricky for those afraid of heights. You could see all the way up and down the building through the breach between the wall and the elevator box. The gap on the sides was wider than the break you step over at the floor of it, and you could see a light bulb burning and the dirty cords and chains. If you looked down the opening in the floor before the door closed on you, you could see about one million bank deposit slips on the basement floor. There was a manual gate that held you in and the dusty concrete walls straggled by you as you went from floor to floor. I always hopped across the brass threshold so a spider wouldn't fall on my shoulder.

As Rosemary pulled Caroline in the elevator, the youngster accidentally turned loose of Barbie's sidekick Skipper that she was holding by the hair. Skipper in her smart little sailor suit hit smack dab on the crack, wiggled, and fell on down the shaft. Rosemary tugged the child harder and warned her to come completely across the void. Caroline bit her lip and tried to keep from going in when her mother dragged her on across. A man politely closed the metal folding fence. After the outer, large steel doors met, there was a moment of rising motor noise and the elevator began to lift.

About the time the floor lights above the elevator doors moved to 2, a radiance began to beam through the crack in the door. I felt a buzzing in my head as the glow floated downward. I knew the gleaming mixture of light wasn't that old 60-watt Sylvania light bulb dangling by the chains. It was a mixed hue of chartreuse and yellow like the angels I'd seen flying towards the building from the ice plant. I did not know why they were going down.

The only place to go below the first floor was the basement. So, I figured there must be a bank robber hiding down in the halls below, because everything was so calm above it. It gave me the shivers and a patch of chill bumps came up on my arms.

When I remembered Maraeze telling me to change out fear for love and I would be protected, I shook it off. Thinking about how much I loved Packy, got up my courage and I sneaked down the green marble stairs to the basement. There was nothing there but a snack machine with Lance crackers and peanut logs and the door to the elevator shaft. The cement hall to the boiler room and the old white drinking fountains were empty and still. Every movement I made echoed in tight, tiny sounds. I turned to the basement elevator doors and tried to pull them apart. My fingers barely fit in-between the rubber sealing.

Wiggling my fingers to get a firmer hold, a small light broke between the doors. The glow from the shaft became even brighter, and I stumbled back as an angel opened the door for me and my eyes felt pinched with the intense brightness. She left it pushed ajar. I would never have been able to open that big steel door alone, and I believe it was bolted up before.

Despite the glaring light, I caught sight of Skipper amongst the papers. Then my brain felt like a plane was taking off in it.

The next thing I knew little Caroline was lying amidst all the papers with her arms and legs going ever' which a way like a rag doll. Rosemary's scream echoed down the shaft and awakened me from gaping at Caroline. I looked up but could see nothing but the angels' light. It was then that I realized Caroline had fallen through the side breach from a higher floor. I heard a piercing metal screech and the lights dimmed as they shut down the power to the elevator.

As I entered the shaft the angels loomed overhead without expression. They looked at me as if I should know what to do. I may have been a child myself but I felt like there was something there I needed to protect. I bore deep respect for Caroline, and she somehow seemed courageous and deserving of my deepest admiration. Not much more than a toddler, she plunged to her death with not one whimper of fear or resistance.

Hurt was the last feeling she deserved, or loneliness. If she was feeling pain, the good Lord could just pass it off on me. Cut my pinkie toe off forever without even numbing it would be fine with me, if she could be released from the least pain or discomfort. A baby girl like her should not have to be in a manner like this.

She did not make a motion, even to breathe, and I knew she had been killed instantly. There was a somber heaviness on my chest when I realized this was her time.

She took her sweet little spirit from the place, and the world seemed hollower and more deserted without her. Though I fought the idea of her death for a moment in my mind, rejecting her death grew more pointless and emptier with each new tick of the clock. It was something that could not be taken back, not even if I never disobeyed anyone again in my life.

Wishing she could see her mother one more time, my heart swelled up on me so tight it pushed a tear down my cheek. She looked so sweet. No doubt her mama was going to miss her something fierce.

I knelt down and turned little Caroline over into my lap, wiped the blood from the corner of her mouth and rubbed it off on my blue jeans. Making her as comfortable as I could, I placed Skipper on her chest, and closed Caroline's soft, delicate arms around the little doll.

Together in that last minute, I believe both of our souls began to think of Rosemary, and I could smell Rosemary's perfume rubbed off on Caroline. In my solemn thought, I mulled over what would be the better thing for her mama to do. Wait for her heart to ease with passing time or just come to the knowing that what had happened was somehow what was meant to be.

3

Wershepines Meadow

It took a long time for folks on the first floor to figure out what had happened and for anybody to get down to Caroline and me. I had a little time to memorize her.

She looked to me to be about four or five years old. Her little navy dotted-Swiss dress was high-waisted, with a big navy bow around it, and I smoothed it down for her. She had lacey-topped bobby socks and some black Mary Jane's. A cheap little pin that comes from a gumball machine was pinned on her left shoulder, a ratfink with little blue pants on. There were no freckles to speak of on her little chubby cheeks. Her eyelashes were long and blond like her hair. It looked as if her mother wrapped her hair in a hot iron because it hung down in perfect long ringlets. A beauty mark lay beneath her bottom lip, and I could say a truer mark was never placed. Her lifeless eyes were the blue of a dyed Easter egg and her lids were half open. I took my thumb and pinky finger and tried to shut them down for good, but they wouldn't stay.

She had something on her wrist that was an odd bracelet wrapped around twice. It was thick and had a round red metal tag on it.

The baby girl didn't turn into an angel like Clovis Ray. After her body was quieted for a while, her soul rose up and peered at the angels. She had no wings or anything. About that time, I heard barking and there was a little red weenie dog that jumped out of the wall and started dodging all around her, begging her to play. She gave off an excited little squeal and chased after him with the angels close behind.

The angels didn't tell me squat about what to do with her body from there, so I just kept stroking her little cheek.

When the police guard and bank men in their suits got down the stairs to us, they didn't come into the shaft; they just froze at the threshold. They tried to hold Rosemary back, but released her quickly, not knowing what else to do.

She did not scream Caroline's name or try to wake her. She sat down on the floor and took her from me as gently as you would take a newborn babe. Pulling her close, she placed her head alongside Caroline's and rocked her back and forth and squeezed her tightly, sobbing. Mr. Delaney came into the shaft, but did not interrupt his wife, pacing through the rattling papers, turning his hat brim between his hands like a steering wheel.

It didn't take long for the Justice of the Peace to come to pronounce her dead. It was the first time I had seen him do it without even touching the body. He looked at the child, and then he looked up the shaft and left shaking his head.

Someone had called Packy away from talking over coffee, and he looked puzzled as to how I got down there with Caroline. I told him the truth about looking for bank robbers.

By the time the Justice of the Peace was ready to release Caroline to us, Packy had nearly rubbed my back raw trying to comfort me, though I didn't need consoling. I was making my peace about it. And of course, I was not scared of dead folk, naturally being raised with them in our house. But any sane person is rattled by a life taken, that has not at least ripened to the age of forty years, I'd say. Much less a person that still looks like a baby doll in a department store window.

Rosemary became hysterical in the Cadillac as we drove home afterward, with Caroline covered up with somebody's coat. Packy stopped and we rearranged things with Caroline's head in her mama's lap, no coat, and her feet in my lap. It seemed to suit her mama better, and I was pleased to take her shoes off and rub her little feet.

The nicest part of our home is Prather Funeral Parlor, which is situated to the front. It is unusual even in a small town like

Onward for a death to occur and the family and body to ride to our outfit without the hearse and gurney. But the death of children brings people to their senses and they forget rules that don't make a difference anyway.

Packy kept the bodies of grown-ups in the rooms with plastic accordion doors, but he let dead children be visited at their home. I don't know if it is legal to keep dead folk in their own houses, but Packy says the government does not pay his bills, and he will run his business as he pleases.

While we were riding, Rosemary pulled the bracelet off the baby girl's arm and spoke with halted talking, through her tears. She said the bracelet was nothing but a dog collar from Hoopie, Caroline's dog that died. Caroline used to roll her hula-hoop across the lawn with a stick and Hoopie jumped in and out of it all the way. Hoopie loved it until his back broke down as weenie dogs are apt to do because of their build. She shrugged and said, "We made Caroline give the hula-hoop away. The doctor told us to keep Hoopie from bending at the middle for two weeks and keep him from jumping off the sofa. Caroline would take him off the sofa and he would jump right back up, wagging his tail." She frowned and laughed at the same time, and then started to cry all over again.

"We never told Caroline she probably killed the dog feeding him her barbeque sandwich," she said. Then it appeared, for a moment, too painful for her to explain and we sat in quiet. Even I knew pepper and spices would kill a dog because it attacks their organs worse than chocolate.

Then Rosemary said it was her fault, thinking Caroline could resist Hoopie begging for a bite. She said she wasn't clear to Caroline that Hoopie couldn't eat it, for his own good.

I didn't pipe up to that. I just looked at her with concern and she carefully put the bracelet back on the sweet little arm. She told Packy to leave the dog collar on Caroline, and I knew that was right.

"Calvinia, promise me you won't leave the baby alone ever, and that you will be with her until you bring her home to me." She put her hand up to her mouth to stop herself from crying out again.

"I promise you, Mrs. Delaney, that wild horses could not part us." I was serious and I placed my hand right over my heart.

When we pulled into our driveway, Mr. Delaney was there to take his wife to their house. She put Caroline's hand in mine and kissed both of our hands before she walked to her car. Mr. Delaney had the door open for her, but she did not look him in the eye. She slumped into her seat, and stared blankly forward as they pulled away.

***

Packy tried his best to send me on to do other things, but I wanted to stay with Caroline. He was good about keeping a body covered out of respect, except for the area he was working on. I kept expecting her to say ouch or jump because she looked so young and alive.

She was not like the bodies Packy picks up from the nursing home. They are so stiff that Packy has to break them up in order to straighten their legs and arms out to go in the casket. She turned easily and calmly, like babies when you situate them for a nap.

After Packy prepared her and we got Caroline to her house, her mama went into a crying spell all over again. She cried so long and hard that her lips turned a violet blue before she gasped in air. But when she got some of it out, she stopped jittering so bad and was calmer with Caroline at home. I stayed with Caroline all day, so her mother could come in and out of the room and make arrangements. Packy seemed proud to leave me with Caroline, and talked professional with me, like I was grown.

Bro. Delaney moved around the house like he was some kind of visitor and nothing was wrong. When he brought Caroline's dressing clothes down to our business, he dropped them off like he was the postman with a mail order package. Packy says that's the kind of person that will be a big surprise some day. One minute they are eating a bacon sandwich and the next minute they are on top of a building threatening to jump off, or they'll just haul off and kill somebody.

All the time I was at the Delaney's they seemed to be magnets pushed against matching ends. Each time Bro. Delaney came within six feet of Mrs. Delaney, she went the other way and skirted talking with him or looking at him straight all day. Other than telephone calls she made to relatives and the church, I could not see that she was getting anything done. She tried to straighten up her house in a frenzy, but nothing was out of place and it was sparkling clean.

Before I left the Delaney's house, late afternoon, I helped Rosemary remove the lid, and take the casket from the parlor to Caroline's room. We laid it in her bed and pulled the linens up to cover the bottom half of it, and Rosemary laid on the right side and watched her all night I suppose. She probably played with her hair and smoothed her dress down a hundred times. I wish I had a dollar for every time she told Caroline "baby, I'm sorry," but it wouldn't buy her back.

When I left down the front steps of Caroline's porch, Moody was waiting under a mimosa tree. "Is the baby going to be alright?" he asked.

"She's fine, Moody," I said. "She got picked up by the angels."

He looked right satisfied when I told him that. Anybody else would have gone to pieces like that was a bad thing.

"She is going to live with Jesus?" he asked, still needing some reassurance.

"Yep, Jesus, and her little dog, Hoopie, that died here 'while back, not to mention all the angels."

"Lucky duck," Moody offered.

A glimmer caught my eye, and I reached down to pick me up a little piece of orange glass. I had never seen broken orange glass before. Moody jumped like I was fixing to toss a rock at him.

"I ain't going to throw a rock at you, Moody."

He didn't say anything. He just hopped twice on his back leg, stuck the right one forward, straight as a board, tipped forward and kept on going like nothing happened.

"You can walk with me to Wershepines Meadow if you want to, but that is as far as your mama wants you to go, Moody, you know that."

"Not if I am with you, Cal."

"Yeah, but then I would have to walk you back and that defeats the purpose. You can play at my house some time. Tara won't care. Packy won't care."

"Can we go down to the Sabine River Bottom?" he asked me.

Now that is my private place. Lord, are you going to make me treat him like a king? Am I still making up for saying the word retard? Never mind, it ain't my river bottom no ways and it is always right to share. I turned and looked him over from head to toe. He looked nervous, putting his hands back and forth in his pockets. The corners of his mouth bounced up and down, like he couldn't control whether he would be straight or grin. I think if I said something ugly about him, it would hurt him real bad. Most of all it would hurt him because he would believe it.

"You got any play clothes?"

"What do you mean?"

"Like tenny-shoes. Like short-legged britches, the real kind and a T-shirt or something?"

"Maybe." He looked like he had no idea but would look real hard.

"Well put some on and tell your mama you are having supper with me and we will go down to the Sabine River Bottom before dark." He froze for a minute in his path like he was in shocked surprise. And then his motor started turning.

"Hurry," I said.

I should have known better than to ever say hurry to Moody. He started to take out running. Then he realized he was going the wrong way, turned too fast and fell flat on his face. He jumped up and took out again in the right direction and saluted me when he went by. If there are crowns in heaven for doing good works like the Baptists say, mine will be so heavy it will cripple my neck.

When I got home, I don't think Packy would have said no to me if I had asked to take the Cadillac to New York City. Tara had her nose so far in the ironing that she was dropping sweat on it.

Tara was so big she never even knew when she was pregnant. The doctor said the fat squeezed down on her female organs so hard that her monthly visitor didn't come very regular and sometimes not at all. She would tell Packy her back was hurting her and leave work early. The next day she would send one of her boys by to say she'd be late because she'd had a baby.

Tara's mother on the other hand was scared to death of having babies. Birthing hurt so bad she held Tara in the womb for almost a year and a half. Black babies are usually born light colored and turn darker over time. When Tara was born, she had long hair, and they had to clip her fingernails the first day they were so grown out. She was already black as tar and that's why they named her Tara. The doctor had to take her mama to the Black hospital and knock her unconscious before he could get Tara out. When he spanked Tara, she cried out and he saw that she already had her two front teeth. Her mama wouldn't let her nurse because of the teeth and they say Tara ate a chicken leg before she ever left the hospital. And believe you me that Tara has been eating ever since.

She goes to an awful lot of trouble to straighten her hair out and keep it from breaking off. Packy said White folks wash the grease out of their hair, but Black folks have to put grease back in it. He supplied no reasoning for this and he would not let me clarify such with Tara.

It hurts me to see the ordeal of Tara combing her hair because she acts like her head is on fire and she is trying to put it out with the comb. She breathes real heavy like her arms are tiring and she has to rest for spells until she gets it whipped down. She keeps it oiled and combed flat and then curled up right on the ends to where it looks like a Roman soldier helmet. Sixty-five mile-an-hour winds would not have swayed it.

When Packy described her, he said she was as wide as she was tall. She wore scuffy house shoes to work and every day of the week but Sunday. I guess she didn't know it but her dresses were not dresses. They were meant to be housecoats like people give you when you go into the hospital. They were short-sleeved cotton that snap all the way up the front with a flower pattern. But it made me no difference.

She had a smart little grin on her face when I said I had a boy coming to supper. Making the table a little fancier than usual, I knew she was pleased to show off the art of her cooking. She slyly commented that it was too early for me to have an interest in boys. And what she meant by interest I have no idea, because I didn't think of him like a good book or a piece from a museum.

I ate myself some fried okra, black-eyed peas and honeydew melon. But Moody was so excited he could barely choke anything down, and he kept making all kind of roller coaster movements with his fork. He couldn't just bring the fork straight to his mouth. His arm must have had a mind of its own so that Moody had to catch the bite in midair. I don't know if that was spastic coming out or he was just like that from watching too much television.

I was obliged to watch the fork though, to keep from looking at the black socks he had on with his sister's size ten and a half twirler shoes. He had on some tight blue jean shorts that were hemmed with a cuff like a girl's too. The T-shirt was a daddy undershirt. *Next time I am going to keep my mouth shut.* He looked better with the tie on.

When Packy said we could be excused, Moody turned his water glass over and stood up so quick he knocked his chair on its back. But not before the water hit him right between the legs, and of course, it looked like he peed.

"Young lady, don't let me catch you near no Sabine River Bottom," Tara demanded as we popped open the screen door.

"Don't worry, you won't," I answered truthfully. She wouldn't because she was too scared to go down there.

"The wild woman eats up road kill and any kind of baby rabbits or squirrels," Tara said in a warning voice. She came to the back porch and opened the screen door and looked at us with authority. Then she began to talk slower like we were not understanding.

"She will eat a nest of new baby rats still pink and hairless." After that statement, she nodded and stepped back holding the screen door, in case we needed room to run back in the kitchen screaming. When that didn't work, she added more story to it.

"Parrish Carlisle will tell you she is a thief. He left his boy's purple heart on the front porch swing, and when he went back out to get it, it was gone. Tell me he ain't got no reason to be afraid." She cocked her head convincingly and lowered one eyebrow.

When she got to talking about the wild woman, sometimes her eyes popped out like jumbo marshmallows with a Hershey's kiss stuck up in them. Then her vessels bulged and she got woozy. She had to line up with a chair just right to sit down, and it almost tipped backwards from her weight. She looked like she was just squatting halfway to the floor, because you couldn't see the chair, once she sat down and her skin draped over it.

But there was something funny about her stories because, number one, I didn't know how she would know anything about the wild woman, being too scared to ever go around her. Number two, if it weren't for the wild woman, Parrish Carlisle would never have let the Black people squat on his land. Then where would Tara have lived with all her boys? So, to my way of thinking she should have let the stories be, but she was hypnotized every time the wild woman's name was mentioned.

Tara lived with her family down in Wershepines Meadow, which we would pass through going to the Sabine River Bottom. Dr. Parrish Carlisle told the Black folks they could stay on his land down in the parts close to the Sabine, for free, as long as they would see after him. They could build, plant, and do as they please. So, they took him up on it.

Wershepines was not the official name on a map or anything. Parrish, a used-to-be surgeon turned hermit, made that promise to the Black folks the first time they came calling on him in search of work. He said, "I don't have any work for you, but you can squat down there in the meadow where she pines." It was in reference to the wild woman and that's how it stuck. Come to find out later he was glad to have them because he did not want to be alone, so close to where the wild woman lived. For Parrish, the fear of the wild woman was paralyzing.

It was a good thing the Black folks cared for Dr. Carlisle or he would have shriveled up and died. Tara and her people kept him supplied with vegetables and ham pieces, bacon, eggs and what not. They said he eats like a bird and his bones have rubbed out white patches on his pants like a snuff can. The only way to see him is through the screen door. He throws a rope out that is hitched to a little red wagon and he pulls it in if he is satisfied the coast is clear.

He was even afraid to take out the trash to burn or stack it for Tara's people. There was a terrible raccoon problem at his house because he just threw scraps off the back porch to keep the house from smelling so. Coons would not be such pesky varmints if God had not given them hands with a working thumb.

***

The sun had retreated from the pasture and broke the scorching heat to a bearable, sultry breeze. My nose wrinkled with the strong smell of musty, dry weeds, and I looked forward to the wilted scent of the wet oak and vines of the Sabine River Bottom. I went down the porch two steps at a time.

"Where are we headed?" Moody asked with a hint of mischief in his voice.

"Sabine River Bottom," I said, matter of factly.

"Tara said we couldn't go there, and I know you do what's right, Cal. All the time you do." He said this careful-like, still smiling with hope.

I turned him around right quick because he was going to pay attention. "Listen here, Moody," I said holding his elbows. "She said she didn't want to *catch us* at the Sabine River Bottom; there's a difference."

"Oh," he said nodding as if he was soaking it in. "You are the smartest girl I know, Cal." He smiled big, like a choking cat.

"She would have to come down there to catch us, right?" I looked back over my shoulder to bear out what I was saying and size up my new friend. I was talking a little lower for no particular reason.

Different or not I liked Moody. And what was I thinking about different? "All God's children," I repeated as Tara always said to me."

"Right," Moody said, just agreeing with anything I uttered. I started two-stepping and skipping then to hurry on. When I looked back over my shoulder to make sure Moody was keeping up, I glimpsed Evangelise coming from back over behind our house towards us. With the excitement of seeing her, I missed a skip and fell flat to my knees. I watched her wing, all the way across the pasture, while I dusted up dirt trying to get to my feet. Moody finally pulled me up by the hand.

"Race!" I said, to pick up Moody's pace. A burst of energy came over me and I plunged down the path in a dead run. I could hear Moody's twirler shoes tapping the path right behind me.

4

The Pirates

Moody's legs were so long I took three steps to every one of his lanky, prancing steps. He was always turning his ankle but never broke it. I knew he was enjoying himself, which made me feel good. But I could not explore with Moody while there was an angel in Wershepines Meadow.

Buzzards were circling high above in the distance, doing their ritual dance. A cruel sign, they begin this party for some kind of death. I do not like buzzards, and they are the only birds in Wershepines that are as ugly as lye soap. They have long crooked necks, and they look like moth eaten rugs where there are clumps of feathers missing. Packy says they are the clean-up crew and a necessary part of life. I know they are just waiting until mightier animals eat to their fill before it is safe for them to land and clean the bones. They celebrate the likely stillborn calf, or perhaps an old cow bogged down in the deep pond mud.

Evangelise would be at risk for sinking if she warned me about anything, so I didn't even try hollering at her. I kept on moving until I could see the dense trees outlining the river.

As we made our way farther, I saw some tracks and the dry grass was trampled down like somebody had been driving in circles on it. The patterns were fresh which caused me to pause and try and sum it up. Miller High Life bottles were scattered all around. We came to a cluster of tall, gray anthills, mashed almost flat with narrow tire treads across them. The tall line of oak and pecan trees stand witness to this meadow and have for a hundred years, but cannot testify to what has happened here.

My good sense told me to turn and go back home, but my heart's desire was to see the angels whenever I could bring my mind to clearness. I hesitated a moment, and thought about whether I should move forward. Once I glimpsed Evangelise again ahead of us, there was no doubt I would continue following her. I turned to Moody, "Let's be Indian scouts," I told him.

When I started creeping forward, Moody started sidling as my shadow. I was pleased, because that way I didn't have to tell him what to do. I tried to keep us as low to the ground as I could. The milkweed we crawled through made us sticky but it kept us hid.

I was troubled but not afraid because the Sabine River Bottom was my paradise. It is a wonderland for playing and discoveries. Sitting in front of the television does not compare to the fun I have when I am at the river. I have axed me off two or three big vines from the trees hanging out over the Sabine and I swing out on them like Tarzan. The treetops are like a porte-cochere over the top of the river because it is narrow and the branches hide the river from the sky. At the end of Wershepines Meadow, the drought has made the Sabine so skinny, I can almost throw a rock and hit the other side. The dry summer season had shrunk the river and it no longer flowed in waves. Rows of cow prints were deep and dried like clay art from the receded shoreline of spring. Water barely tumbled over flat, mossy rocks in the deep green bath. You could not see fish, or even sticks after they went under an inch or two. Water bugs made wakes like tiny motorboats in their crazy circles.

Each time I used the same dangling vines because they are settled. The first time you swing out on a new one they can untangle off the end and not swing back. Then you have to drop into the murky river. I never axed off new vines in the wintertime.

Nearing the bank, I heard voices and men's angry laughter, like they were not laughing in fun. Moody was solemn and he didn't make a peep. I don't know what kind of grades Moody makes, but on reading the lay of things he seems kind of smart.

The wheel tracks matted down the meadow grass, and we followed their trail to the rising at the river's edge. Closer to the shore, we jumped over on the cow path. The path is smoothly worn with no weeds where cattle and horses go down to water, and we inched down it quietly. I motioned to Moody to stay put so I could sneak up to the big rooted cypress tree and get a look at the men behind the voices.

On the riverbank, I could see a bunch of menfolk around a campfire with tattoos on every inch of their skin. They wore bandanas and earrings and had their pants tucked into their high-top boots. Looked to me like maybe they were pirates but there was no boat that I could see. But there were fancy motorcycles with leather fringe hanging off of the handlebars to match their vests that said hell something, but I couldn't make out the other words. The little red devil below it had horns on his head, red wings, a point on the end of his tail, and he was sitting up on a motorcycle. Red and yellow flames were licking at his feet and up the motorcycle and the little devil was smiling fiendishly.

They were all sharing one cigarette. They took a long toke and held their air in as long as they could like puffed-up toads. Then they talked funny as they let it out, like something was cutting their wind off. When it got short, they put it on what appeared to be a pair of scissors but they still cocked their heads and went after it. They were saying words I could never repeat, but will try only to convey their meaning. They were fighting mad that somebody from some other gang had somehow slipped into their fold. I couldn't tell the name of the other gang because half the time they called them Black Knights and then they called them mean and belittling things like butt bandits. They called this Leo guy a fairy, traitor, and south end of a horse. They talked about him like he was gone, and I wondered what happened to him. Then they talked about getting the h.e.double toothpicks out of Dodge City before some more of the dumb son of something come along or some stupid redneck from town wandered by and found Leo. They told the guy they call Red that he really whupped Leo good. Red didn't take kindly to the compliments and told them to shut their southern ends up.

After some time spying on the pirates, and listening to their huffing and bragging, my legs began to get locked up on me. But I was scared to move. The dirt clods under my feet were loose and I feared they would roll down and splash the river water and give away my hiding place. *Lord, don't let Moody take a notion to move over here*, I prayed.

It was starting to get dark, and I saw that Moody's knees were wearing out too, because he was shifting in the grass. He squatted lower and I heard the backside of his shorts give way. The rip was loud. The pirate men hushed up and looked over towards us. I could see a topaz glow from the treetop spill down on my shoulders.

All of a sudden, a coon shot down the tree and took out running right past the pirates. They tried to grab their Bowie knives and whatever they could throw to strike but nobody got close to hitting him. I knew it was not very likely for a racoon to come down a tree and run at people.

They were quieter for a while and I watched them go back to sharing their one cigarette. When the light of dusk was no longer, the only brightness came from their campfire. I knew they couldn't see out into the darkness, so I decided it was time to make my move. I pondered a moment on my options. If I made a noise, they might kill me, I knew that. If I didn't get Moody back soon, Packy would certainly kill me. That was a sore place to be in.

When I pulled my leg around to turn and skulk out from the roots of my hiding place, dirt clods rolled in a small avalanche down the steep shore. When the clods hit water, it sounded like somebody doing a can-opener into the river. The pirates left their Bowie knives in their leather slips and pulled guns out from their pants and boots, then hunkered down. I didn't know whether to make a run for it or fake death.

My breath was stuck. I closed my eyes because there was a feeling in my heart like I was fixing to go straight to heaven and my head and ears rang a bit.

About that time, an agonizing wail built to a shrill screech and trumpeted from the treetops. Then the pirates really started shuffling, and I could hear the movements of their boots. A sizzling sound of sand and water being thrown on the fire came next and the light dimmed. Fear leaked out my toes, and I just stood right up and turned around facing them, though I could only see their silhouettes in the moonlight. Moody was already on his feet. A flashlight scanned the bank and angled across my body illuminating my and Moody's eyes like a couple of wild cats.

Then they jerked back to the sound echoing about that was like what I have heard before when Packy and I come up on coyotes or a pack of wild dogs. We have heard it in the distance when we have gone out frog gigging late at night. It was similar to the sound of a rabbit with its foot caught in a coon trap.

The echo seemed to meander around the campfire as if it was coming from no particular direction, followed by a ghostly echo. I would not repeat all the cussing that went on at that point. Suffice to say I heard every word I knew and then some.

Suddenly from the far side of the pirates, a silhouette flew from the trees and jumped straddle-legged right over the embers of their campfire. The shape was a small Indian shadow or possessed thing with something like burlap sacks flowing from its body and tassels from its head.

I ducked back down. The pirates started shooting up the place trying to hit it, and one of the pirates took the Lord's name in vain and said, "You stupid children without a real daddy, I'm hit. Let's get the you-know-what out of here!"

The silhouette disappeared as quickly as it came. The pirates jumped on their motorcycles and drove off without their lights on. When they got up the river bank and about a quarter mile off, they hit their lights. Revving their motors, they were soon out of sight. All the pirates and motorcycles were gone, including the pirate that got hit. A glow in the air above the path leading home made me know it was safe to leave.

We were so shaken we were silent. I had my head down making good time and Moody bounced along behind me as if he was waiting for me to say something.

I thought perhaps I was spared from the pirates for a special purpose, but then I decided that I was putting on airs to think I could do missions like that of the angels. Maybe God was just saying thank you to me for helping little Caroline.

"I think those men might hurt us if they had caught us, Cal," Moody offered softly. "I don't think those were nice men."

"No, Moody, they weren't." I stopped a moment and straightened up and talked to Moody like he had some sense. "So that is why you can only go to the Sabine River Bottom, with me, you hear? Don't ever go down there without me."

"Yes, Cal."

"This is our place, Moody, our secret. And if you tell anyone, you can't go with me again, you understand?"

"Yes, Cal, I understand, and I promise." He offered me his hand. I would have pricked our fingers and mixed our blood to seal it, but I am waiting on the age of twelve when Packy says I can have a pocket knife.

A trip that takes a usual thirty minutes seemed only to take us five. Packy was waiting on the porch with his hands on his hips.

"What have y'all been doing?" Packy asked. He was to the point, but he didn't sound mad. It wasn't like it was a school night. I figured I was still getting some slack for being good to Caroline.

"Hiding," I said.

"Hiding?"

"Yessir, Cal ain't lying to you, Mr. Prather. We were hiding," Moody said earnestly.

"Well, that's fun, children," he said with a smile. "Say, Moody, I'm going to run you home now, fellah, if that's all right. Cal, would you go fetch the keys?" Packy asked me.

"My mama can come and get me, Mr. Prather. You don't have to go to trouble," Moody offered. "I'm not scared to walk home either."

"Well, I talked to your mama, and it sounds like she wants you home here pretty quick. She didn't sound like she was in any shape to drive when I spoke to her, Moody. I 'spect I better run you over." Packy looked off to the side like it was no big deal about Moody's mother being drunk.

When I came back to the porch with the keys, I could hear a rattletrap car coming down the road. The car squeaked and rocked when it hit the least little bump, and veered from side to side like a boat in storm-tossed waters. Pulling up in front of the house, Moody's mama must have hit the gas and the brake at the same time because the motor raced even though it was locked up. The old Ambassador died after a few sputtering jerks. She reached down, butting her head against the steering wheel and then twisted off her high heel and threw it against the passenger door, blaming it for the pedal misfortune. She cracked her door open to turn the lights on inside and I could see her searching, mumbling something about her cigarettes.

My mouth fell open when I saw that she was wearing nothing but a fire engine red underslip with the strap hanging down. Long stringy blades of hair hung forward and a nest matted up at the back of her head in one massive knot. It was black in some places and red in others with a mousy brown row down the roots. Mascara circled her eyes like a bandit, and she wore smeared lipstick and a beauty mark she had painted on herself.

She wrestled her sun visor halfway out the window and was trying to get under it enough to yell at Moody. "Thank the kind folks, Moody, and let's get home." She said it sweetly, like a sad-faced clown with her eyes almost closed. Then her head gave way like Packy's does when he falls asleep in the porch swing. It snapped against the visor and made her mad. She went to swatting at it and tried to pull it out of the way and smacked herself good with the end coming back the other way. That made her go crazy, so she started slapping at it and yanking at it to pull it completely off. She managed to bend it. Then she started wrenching it around and around trying to wear it down so it would come loose. We had time to go pop some corn and come back for the finish. Packy scratched his head and looked at me from time to time like he thought he should say something, lifting up his heels, and then his toes. He smoothed his beard and folded his arms and opened and closed his mouth several times, with no words coming out.

Moody shifted from his front leg to his back leg, to and fro wanting to help her but not knowing quite what in the heck she was doing.

She finally wrenched it off and threw it out in our yard. We all nodded like we were glad she had so aptly finished the job. "Won't you come in a spell and have a cup of coffee, Jewel?" Packy asked politely.

I bit my bottom lip to keep from smiling. I couldn't wait to see the look on Packy's face when she stepped out of her car half naked in her underslip.

"No, no," she said. "Coffee keeps me awake."

"Well," Packy said. "That might be a good thing while you're driving."

Squinting back up at Packy, it looked like her head was swimming and her eyes were rolling to focus. "Well fancy that," she wrinkled her nose up and shrugged her shoulders, "an undertaker who's a part-time comedian." She smiled and leered at Packy for a moment. "Get in the car, Moody," she said with no patience.

Moody jumped for the door. You could see the white of his panties out the back of his sister's shorts. He went to pulling at the door like somebody was fixing to get him, trying to mind his mother. There was jerking and snapping with his hand flying off the handle. His mama just sighed and reached back over the seat and unlocked the door. Humbly, he pulled it open.

When Jewel had backed up and gone forward umpteen times in ample space to turn around, she finally nosed through our gate to leave. She took our mailbox down with the front bumper. It got pushed up under her car making a dragging, scraping sound and she pulled it halfway to the highway.

Packy seemed in deep thought, and he didn't even say anything about her tearing up our mailbox. He looked to be in thoughts from another time, another place.

"Packy." I interrupted his thinking.

"Yeah," he said a little jumpy, like he forgot I was there.

"Ain't you scared for them to go off like that? Ain't you scared she is going to get them run off in a ditch or that they'll run down a cow or something."

"I might be." He said it like it was something he couldn't help.

"Well, why didn't you try to stop her, Packy? I am getting to like ol' Moody, ain't you?"

"I don't ever want to be part of something, Calvinia, that is not born of good judgment. I want to do right whenever and wherever I can. I have to tell you there are parts of me that wanted to yank her out of the driver's seat and give her a good talking to." He looked down at me as though admitting a weakness, but then he peered off in the distance.

"But if I did, I would be taking matters into my own hands, and that isn't right because that would be tangling things up in my fears. That wouldn't do them or me any good. It would be like saying I don't believe God can watch over Moody and his mama with the same mercy we are cared for. I have no control over her situation, I must accept that. If something I think is bad comes of it, I have to know that in the long run, it will turn out best for all concerned."

Packy smiled down at me and I smiled back. He patted me on the back and led me into the house with him. In our nightly prayers, we prayed for God to watch over and keep Moody and his family safe, and soothe Jewel's painful heart. Packy ended his prayer by saying, "And please God, help Cal to stop saying ain't."

5

Leo the Lion

I was sitting up under a bowl, and that Tara was cutting my hair to look like the little boy on the Buster Brown shoebox. She thinks I am the spitting image of him and should do commercials my ownself. I was trying to hold still so it wouldn't look like my hair got cut with pinking shears.

She knows I like to go barefoot and to me dresses are of no count. I prefer a sailor hat, cut-offs and a pretend cigar stick in my mouth any day to some fancy pinafore-topped outfit. I would just as soon cut a hole for my head in a tablecloth and wear it, I think dresses are so silly.

Packy wants me to be a lady and Tara knows just how far we can push him. She will let me know when she feels we have reached his limits. I used to wear a dress to school every day. But Tara has finally settled Packy for me to wear britches on Tuesday and Friday, or any day that bumps up against a holiday.

Tara teaches Sunday School, is a godly woman and a teetotaler. She always announces nice and loud to her church lady friends that she only buys and transports liquor for Dr. Parrish and does not partake in it herself. I said she better not because she is always pregnant. She would be drinking for two. Her deaconess position at the Rose of Sharon Church would also be in jeopardy if she drank liquor.

And I would hate that because I would go to church with her sometimes on Sundays. I liked Black churches because they are natural born singers and they don't just sing it, they holler it. Best thing is, the singing takes up most of the church time. White people liked to hear themselves talk too much.

White people think you have to have a husband in the house too, or it ain't right. Black people rightly leave it up to choice. If you have the rare man who brings home his earnings and shares your view of worship, raising children, and the good book, then sure why not marry? But if you just have a grown child that needs to be waited on, and that dips into your flour can for spending money, may as well raise your kids by yourself. That way your offspring will be fit to marry and have children of their own. A fair warning to any man that might want to court Tara; don't say a cross word to or about one of her boys if you like having a head between your shoulders.

Other kids in my class may have a lady like Tara at the house one day a week or maybe two. But nobody gets to have someone every day but Sunday. And for sure not someone who can put their foot down, warn the teacher not to paddle you, and help you through your life like Tara. And for double sure, not someone to tell you what happened to your mama and grandmother when it pains your Packy to blubbering tears ever' time a name is mentioned. I can say every word she told me by memory, and every move she made is in my head like a roll of film.

Tara took my hand between her hands like a sandwich, and looked directly into my eyes. "Don't nobody leave this earth until they mission is finished," she told me. "And your mama and your grandmother Mims, finished this job here on earth at the same time." She nodded so that I knew she stood behind every word she said.

"They went into the water brave as any soldier to war, and their bodies did not rise up. Not in time to breathe. And when they came out, they soared up out of that water together, and went on up to be with Jesus."

She smiled a little softer when she saw me ease that she said they were with Jesus. She pulled my hand closer and tighter and made sure I was still able to listen.

"Some people call it drowning. I call it being baptized into heaven. Whatever they had to accomplish was simply done.

And they awarded your Packy the most precious gift anyone could give. And that was the job of raising you."

Tara may repeat their story again from time to time, but we don't speak about my father. That is because Packy and Tara feel it is a danger to me. Explaining it to me further just makes me more likely to get hurt, in many ways, they tell me. They always hush me up from questions in a way that I know they will not budge.

I figure he is probably a spy and everyone has to keep his job a secret for both our safety. Could be royalty or something and someday this will come to light. Was it that he doesn't know where I am and would steal me away from them? Maybe. Or, might be he did something bad and they don't want me caught up in it. I like to think of all the reasons this situation has to be a secret we can't talk about. At times, I come up with some real humdingers that involve his kidnapping by gypsies, or not returning from a safari and what not. But there is no moving them yet about that conversation.

I have at times fit in the question to just ask them if they know where he is. They always say "we don't know at the moment." This could mean he is just outside, but we don't know on which side of the house, or could mean we don't know if he is on the ground, in the air or in some foreign country. They leave themselves a lot of room for making their story.

Tara got her laundry sprayer and wet my hair down a little more. I watched her concentrate on the job like pleasing me meant something. She cut the back of my hair last and pulled out both sides to compare the lengths. Then she combed it and cupped it into place looking satisfied.

Stepping back to admire her finished art, she handed me a mirror. As I looked at the back of my head, I could see the reflection of a familiar car drive up. It was the county medical examiner.

I knew what that meant. Somebody with no money had died and they wanted Packy to fix them up for a pauper's funeral. Packy said we made about enough money from the government on a pauper case to fill the hearse with gas, and that's about all. "Praise the Lord for a tank of gas," he said, and then went on like they were paying in cash.

Hair went flying everywhere when I threw the towel off my shoulders and Tara started scrambling. "Young lady!" Tara's voice sounded disappointed, but not surprised. The county coroner deliveries are always more interesting, like folks being dead a long time before being discovered, suicides, and illnesses for which they never saw a doctor. Pauper cases mean they are either the poor, the deserted or both. Packy says they are sadder circumstances and are not pampered in death like folks with money. He vows that they will not be discarded once they meet our doors. And I don't want the coroner's helper to leave before I get out there, because he always carries Clove chewing gum.

Packy asked me to hold the door so he could help the deputy because the corpse was a pretty good-sized man. When Packy began to unzip the bag, I saw tattoos all down the arms. They were every kind of lion you could think of, in every different position. There was a mighty lion that was roaring. There was another with a motorcycle jacket on, smoking a cigarette. Some were sitting, some were standing, but they were all looking like they were King of the Jungle.

"Leo the lion," Packy read from a tattoo and I 'bout dropped my teeth out.

This is the guy! I say to myself. Those pirates killed him. I couldn't find my senses for a minute and my mind was going ninety to nothing.

"Looky here, Calvinia." Packy had Leo on the porcelain table, and he was finding Leo to be an interesting case. He had all kinds of marks where he was whipped up on and places that would need a powerful lot of stitches if he had made it. "Coroner took a while to realize what got this fellow."

Packy turned his head a little to the side and I could see what Packy was talking about. Someone had put a gun to his head but they had placed it so far into his earhole to pull the trigger that it was hard to know that he got shot in the head. But a little jellied gray matter leaked out when Packy turned it to the side. The bullet itself probably went to pieces inside the head because there was no place where it left out.

"Poor fellow," Packy said sorrowfully. "He was doing the best he could." Packy pulled a clean cover up over him and began to prepare his instruments.

"What do you mean, Packy?" I beseeched him.

"No telling what has happened to this man in his lifetime to pick this way of living and end up like this. Cold on some slab in a strange town, no family close enough to know the difference. Daddy or Mama might have beaten him when he was little so he puts himself in a place to get beaten again because it's all he knows. They probably told him he wasn't worth shooting and he believed them."

"You mean he had rotten parents, Packy?"

"No, I can't say they were rotten. But his parents' mamas and daddies probably did the same things to them. They were doing all they knew how to do. Thing is, somebody has got to break that chain."

"And be good to their kids like you are to me, Packy?"

"Got to love 'em."

"Like you love me?"

"Just like Packy loves you, Cal."

He picked me up and squeezed me tight and then he looked me in the eye before he kissed me on the cheek. I knew he was examining me to make sure I was alright with seeing Mr. Leo in such a state.

Packy's love for me was plain for all to see, because he never could look me in the eye like that without little tears twinkling over his bottom lids. And as late afternoon as it was, he began to prepare Mr. Leo. This was on the outside chance a family member came, in hopes of seeing their loved one, one more time.

***

Packy had Tara wash out Mr. Leo's own clothes so he could be buried in what he was comfortable in. He trimmed up his beard and shaved off the rough edges where he looked close to handsome, despite the cuts and bruises. Packy didn't have to do such nice things for the paupers because it was not part of the deal. He did it because he wanted to.

I went to my toy box and got out my entire tea set and dishes. Tara made me up some fresh tea and gave me some cookies and I had a pretend tea party with Mr. Leo. I wanted him to do something nice before he went on his way and know that he was welcome in our home. His fingers were nice and stiff and held a cup between them pretty level. I told him I knew he was doing the best he could, and not to worry because what he did was just part of the plan and how things work here on earth.

Right in the middle of my talking I had a flush like maybe I had eaten too much sugar. I got lightheaded and starry-eyed. When it cleared, I saw the chubby angel struggling to keep her height looking down on me and Leo. It was the magenta angel with the low deep voice that I saw with Maraeze. When she realized I had discovered her, she kind of looked embarrassed and lifted off with a little grunt. She was smiling though, and she looked proud like Packy.

6

The Miracle of Fanny J. Crosby

I can smell the fall when it is near. Briskness has a fragrance and the flowers and grass change their mind about living. No longer parched their stems are filled with cool rainwater and they hoard their ration proudly. The sun no longer blisters me and I don't know how it can be so bright yet only caress me.

Autumn leaves begin the cycle of feeding the trees they fell from and the aroma is like new life. Souls are forgiving and endings are brought about in a period of rest before starting again with the new. Morning glories begin their cadence as they rise in the morning and bow at night to the Almighty. Vines go unnoticed until their season and are blessings for which we are only thankful now and then.

—Rev. C. J. Ellison, Tent Revivalist

It was in the fall that Rosemary Delaney prepared to join her Caroline. Her grief was so overbearing that she was succumbing to the struggle that living brought her. Her illness did not get her down with Caroline alive. Without Caroline, the disease was beginning to wreak its havoc on her lungs. The steroids that only made her chubby before made her tired and worn and think only of that which makes you sad.

Her life with Bro. Delaney was a captive hell, and it would be easier for her to give up herself than to stand up and claim any joy. He decided to become ordained so he could spread his fire and brimstone regularly, but did not have a church home as yet. The drawing of his face and his skinny skulking body made church panels think he had one foot in the grave and the other on a banana peel. He left his previous job knowing the Lord would provide for him to do the Lord's work. If the Lord was providing for him, it was being done through Rosemary's parents because the Delaneys had long ago gone broke at the bank where little Caroline passed on.

One Saturday, Packy saw Rosemary's name on a patient admission roster when he went to the hospital. They had called him to the morgue there to pick up the body of a man who had run over himself with his own tractor. I was pleased he thought a visit from me would do her some good.

In her hospital bed, Rosemary looked to me like some kind of war victim at the wax museum. She had an oxygen hose in her nose and it was causing her nostrils to crack open and scab over and she was as pale as Robin Hood flour. Her eyes had no sign of life to them and were empty like a bird's nest with no eggs or little chicks. Her pupils drew up with pain and the knowing that she would never see herself again in pleasure.

Bro. Delaney was an outsider in her room. She closed her eyes tight for his loud prayers that had nothing to do with her condition or comfort and all to do with his repeat message of repenting. It was strange to me that anyone could think that frail little bird had one thing to repent about, and I knew God loved her like a newborn baby.

Bro. Delaney reminded her that her chores were piling up at home and demanded that she quit the chicanery of pretending illness and get back home to her wifely obligations. He was performing duties a man should not have to undertake. He did not want her to get spoiled because of being waited on. She was not the virtuous woman the Bible would describe whose price was far above rubies.

I remembered Tara taught me never to say anything to anybody I would not say in front of Jesus himself. So, I had nothing to say to Bro. Delaney, and matter of fact, holding it back gave me a touch of vertigo. I wanted to defend Rosemary and let him know she was a jewel in my eyes.

Bro. Delaney did not acknowledge my presence in the room at the hospital. But I do believe he felt he had to either tone down his preaching with a child present or go on home. Lucky for me, he chose the latter.

My head started humming and I felt my state coming on before Mr. Delaney ever left the grounds. The minute the door was closed as he was gone, the angels were idling above us looking sweetly upon Rosemary. One was Maraeze, and I heard her call the hefty, magenta angel Belliza, and with them was a third angel who was nothing but white and brighter white. I think her eyes were closed in prayer, but I could not see them behind the tiny round lenses of her dark spectacles. Sweet chords of heavenly music sprinkled down on us that sounded like the tickling of harp strings.

"Speak to her of music," Maraeze beckoned me. Belliza nodded and it comforted me on.

"I bet your congregation is really missing you, Mrs. Delaney," I offered. I spoke a little soft, but she opened up her eyes for a moment to look at me.

"Rosemary," she said. "Call me Rosemary."

"I say, Rosemary, I bet you would be a sight for sore eyes in the organ loft at your church." I paused and left her some room to talk, but she seemed too weak. "I hear there is only piano since nobody can play the organ like you can."

"They have enough," she said without feeling, "for what it is they need to do." She turned her head and closed her eyes in defeat.

"Oh, but you're wrong, Rosemary," I said with a half chuckle. I moved nervously from foot to foot before I calmed and grabbed her side rail and placed my chin over it to speak more directly. "That music is your ministry. God gave you that talent so you could minister to others. I've been there when you played. You... you can touch folk's hearts in a way that the spoken word may not be heard. It would be a shame to hold back the healing of a heart that needs to hear something from God." I trailed off and gave her time to simmer for a minute.

"My ministry? You really think my playing is a ministry?" She opened her eyes again, looking like she wanted to believe me with all her heart.

"Don't you feel that feeling in your heart, like when you play an old Fanny J. Crosby tune, that God couldn't even put it better? That's because it is God, Rosemary. You are just a part of God coming through." I placed my hand over my heart and then declared it true by motioning the cross over it.

"Are you prompting her, Belliza?" Maraeze asked my magenta friend.

"Do you see me sinking, Maraeze?" she said to the matriarch. "The Spirit speaks through the child." Belliza held her station and may even have risen a pinch.

"Oh, I don't know," Rosemary hesitated.

There is no telling how I remembered the words to the hymn or what gave me the notion, but at that point, I just went to singing, low and gentle. When I was fixing to get stuck for the words the angel in white sang with me.

Pass me not, O gentle Savior,
Hear my humble cry,
While on others thou art calling
Do not pass me by.

Rosemary again closed her eyes. When I finished, she had tears streaming from the corners of her eyes making round wet splotches on the crisp hospital pillow.

"You know," she said. "I always wanted to write a hymn. I wanted to even more after little Caroline died. I didn't want to get famous or make money on it. I just wanted people to get a blessing from it."

"What happened?" I asked her.

"Oh, I started it. But everything seemed to get in the way. It didn't feel right. Somehow, something was missing. I don't know." She looked helplessly away from me, disappointed in herself.

"Do you remember any of how it was going to go?"

"Yes, parts of it," she admitted. "I got new inspiration at times when I thought of Caroline, but I couldn't pick it up again because I always started crying so hard. Well, you know. It made it too painful to try to write it again." She looked down and neatly folded a Kleenex in her hand.

"If I get a pencil and paper, can we scribble some of it down, just while you are thinking about it?" I asked her. I scanned the room quickly to see what I could find.

"I guess so." She hesitated. "Well, do you have the time, dear? Shouldn't you be playing or something?" She said it timidly as if she was not worthy of my time.

"Oh no, ma'am, I don't want to play. This is my special purpose," I beamed.

"Your special purpose?" she said, confirming what she heard.

"Yes, ma'am."

Maraeze looked at me like I might spill the beans and moved her pointy finger from right to left, clicking her tongue at me. I shrugged. If you have a special purpose, you can't help it.

"Well, I'm proud you know your special purpose," Rosemary affirmed. "You keep paying attention to your purpose, dear. You be proud of your special purpose," she said as if I had something she never had. Her head drifted to the side of her pillow and she seemed far away in a trance of proud envy.

I found a number-two pencil stub in the pocket of my overalls, and she had a card from the church where I could write on the back. Every hesitation or block she had was quietly filled with precious whisperings from the angel in white. I didn't even have to translate. It was as if Rosemary could hear the white angel with the ears of her soul.

When she finished what seemed to be the last chorus she slipped into a peaceful sleep. Her breathing was easier and she was calm. The angels had their eyes closed in silent prayers of worship.

"It couldn't be put better," I said out loud, "if it was Fanny J. Crosby herself."

Belliza opened her eyes and looked excited all of a sudden. She started motioning her head sideways towards the white angel, rolling her eyes in the white angel's direction.

"Is that?" I started to ask Belliza, but Maraeze opened her eyes and I clammed up and dropped it.

Belliza tried to slide her head back and nod at me where Maraeze couldn't see her. She put her hand to the side of her mouth and motioned without speaking "Fanny J. Crosby, right there." Then she slipped down about half a notch and snapped her finger as if she regretted saying it.

"Belliza," Maraeze cautioned.

"To God be the glory," Belliza chanted.

Fanny J. Crosby's spirit loomed over Rosemary's head with her face still in the meditation of prayer. Her light fell on Rosemary's face.

After a few solemn moments, I closed my eyes and wiped away a tear. When I opened them again, all were gone but Belliza, who was revving up to lift off, and then she was gone behind them.

***

I met Rosemary every afternoon for the rest of the week. Friday, after school, she was so tired out, she couldn't visit with me. On her bedside table was my pencil nub and a couple of pieces of hospital paper written all over the back. She had scored her song completely through the night. At the top it said, *for Caroline.*

With the softest wind around me
Your embrace I feel is mine
Angel's wings that urge me forward
When the strength I need is Thine
Though the path forever turns me

Without fear thus I do tread
Mindful you, forever with me
My salvation and my stead
Chorus:
Would I take the hand of Jesus?
Harbored on the peaceful shore
I see but the step before me
While he sees forevermore.
Gracious love, oh heavenly being
Blessed with the reach of flight
Then I know the truth of seeing
Savior lead me, precious light
I believe you are my angel
Heavenly gift, unchanging love
Sent to me from realms of glory
'til I join thee there above.

***

The next day I rounded the corner by her hospital room and I could see that her bed had been stripped down. I felt sad. Not that she had gone to heaven, but because the angels didn't call me to be with her when she made her journey. I knew little Caroline must have met her.

"Are you Calvinia?" A nurse in proper white and starched, pointy hat looked down at me. It was the first time I really looked a nurse in the eye that wasn't coming at me with a shot or something.

"Yes, ma'am," I said with all respectfulness.

"Mrs. Delaney left this for you, dear." She handed me an envelope.

"Uh, what do you mean by left it, ma'am?"

"When she left, she asked me to give this to you. Her parents came and took her home to Kentucky last night."

"She's alright?"

"Alright is right! She turned the corner almost overnight when she decided to go with them and take that teaching offer. You know her father is the headmaster of a Christian School and Rosemary is going to teach music there. You would have thought some faith healer came in here and just zapped her out of it." When she said that, she clapped her hands together and nodded her head. "She just turned around, like a miracle."

"And Bro. Delaney?"

"Oh, I totally forgot!" She gave a little smirky laugh. "Well, not my place to notify him."

She smiled at me and hurried on about her work. When I opened the envelope, Rosemary had handwritten the words to her song again, just for me. It was in her own pretty handwriting and she had enclosed a note.

In the note she asked one favor of me. She wanted me just to try piano lessons with Mr. Hubert. If I didn't like them, she said I could quit. And what if it had something to do with my own mission in life? Mr. Hubert, she said, was one of the kindest, most gentle men she had ever known and he had taught her to do some special chording on the organ. She noted Mr. Hubert's talent was especially amazing, because his left leg was partially paralyzed in a car crash. But he worked all the organ pedals with his right foot without missing a beat. She said he was blessed with a God-given talent and she wished I would let him share it with me.

I knew Packy didn't want that, but I was glad she had faith in me. And in the last line she wrote, she thanked me for sharing with her my special purpose.

7

The Mourning Dove

When any two souls share love, it is a mighty powerful thing. Love bears a shield, a field of honor, a sense of wholeness to it. And when that veil is pierced by another, it does not harm the sovereignty of love. It only wounds the one who defies such an honest and holy state.

Hearts are laid open and helpless and the one who dealt the wrong is sentenced to redeem themselves or wallow amongst their shame. But shame itself is a cancer, a pestilence, a thing created outside the soul of God. These elements, from the birthplace of fear, are the sole creation of man, the existence of which heaven will never concede. Why would God taint a holy, spotless mind with such things?

—Rev. C. J. Ellison, Tent Revivalist

When Moody showed up with his new 22 Winchester, something told me *here is trouble.* But I couldn't quite cull out the reason for my lack of ease. Moody's mama told him it was high time for him to learn hunting and other things that normal boys do. I knew he needed to follow through with some kind of game kill, or hold his head down for the duration of her apologetic cussing.

On our quest for Moody's manhood, we stopped by a pond just this side of Wershepines. We strategized on pecan-sized heads that popped up in the mud gravy that was the stale watering hole. We argued about whether the little heads were poisonous water moccasins or harmless mosquito-eating turtles. Soon we saw it didn't matter since Moody couldn't hit the broad side of a barn. We tried to hone Moody's skills on milk cartons but we made no strides. When Moody pulled the trigger, he couldn't help but close his eyes and the barrel dipped and pitched like he was standing upright in a boat.

When you think you are beaten, you are beaten. I can tell you because I have seen it in Moody. The longer it took, the farther he shot away from the willing targets. Cow patties on their sides, an old boot, coffee cans, and a Texas brick were victors over the insides of Moody. "I ain't no good, Cal. I just ain't right. Why ain't I right?" He shook the gun as if he was going to throw it to the ground.

"You're right, Moody. And what is right anyhow? Everybody has to practice. You can't be William Tell on day one, nobody can." He took a little comfort that I didn't come down on him, but he was clearly sunk down on himself.

We walked empty-handed down the dirt road at a snail's pace on our way back to my and Packy's house. Moody hoped for fresh roadkill that he could put a bullet in and claim for a prize.

"Wha'chou laughing at?" Moody asked me.

"I ain't laughing at you, Moody; this ain't funny." Then we looked at a flurrying movement beside us and froze like statues. In our stillness we both heard a rolling coo. Some dry weeds bent and broke and sounded like somebody stirring the grass with a fan.

Then up on the fencepost jumped a mourning dove. Sandy gray and soft as a silk suit for laying somebody out, the feathers looked like velvet. Then the playmate jumped from the brown-eyed Susans and piggybacked and jumped around like they were playing leapfrog.

Since I believed I had had all of Moody's down-in-the-mouth and spirit I could stand, I put my hand out and halted him. The mates were playing so they were not bothered by our presence.

I slipped my hand down the shaft of his Winchester until I felt the slender cage around the trigger. I sneaked down to my knees and brought it over my shoulder to aim. Whether or not I took good aim or not I will never know. When I pulled the trigger, I knew surely the insult of my selfish, thoughtless actions would bring about a death. I got the bird getting ridden just where her legs met her belly and I saw her little toothpick leg distorted in the breeze. She slid gracefully over and fell without a fight to the ground below her. When we got over to her, she didn't even look mad. She fluttered calmly with weakness, and the toes on the blown-up leg looked wilted like a dead spider. Small drops of her blood spilled on the dry grass beneath her.

Sorrow took over me like somebody poured hot cooking oil over my head. Moody cried "Cal, no!" and the mate cooed in crying sounds like he was telling her to stay with him forever. Her leg could have held on better with a piece of Scotch tape than the thread of tender skin and soft feathers of her underside.

Moody picked her up like a broken China doll. By instinct he lightly pressed the area of my thoughtless blast. I prayed her look was forgiving, but was afraid that was the look she was born with. She seemed willing to let us hurt her if we didn't know better.

The mate had the same look on his fixed beaded eyes like they surrendered to the calling of her time. I wanted them to fly angrily at me so they could say what I was, even if it was for Moody I had done it.

Moody was too shocked and sorrowful to move. I took her from him gracefully as if she was a bomb that would explode if I jarred her. When I pressed her to my heart to run with her, the mate jumped behind us from fencepost to fencepost all the way to the house. She was like carrying a delicate piece from a glass menagerie and I thought my bare hands against her would end her life. When we laid her on Packy's porcelain working gurney she was silent and glazed over like she was already seeing the light.

Maraeze could not have come at a worse time. She didn't call me down but she didn't look pleased with me in the slightest.

She hovered in the corner like she had bad news, but the bad news was me and my shunning of my special purpose.

If she had stayed and told me what I did wrong, I would have obediently owned it. Disappointment pressed her on to something of a nobler cause, I knew. I tried to give the mourning dove sugar water from the hummingbird feeder Moody fetched from outside to revive her. But she was without vigor or a cause to rise. Her companion sat on the sill and trilled a feeble coo. My reasoning to save Moody from shame was purely senseless.

The lover seemed to submit to the end of life, as she knew it. She did not resist the calm of a chest closed to new air. She would not take my breath though my spirit was offered up in disgrace.

All I could think to do was run for Packy. I just wanted to be near him, even if it would stoke my shame. He was standing at the altar of the England Grove Baptist Church when I found him. He must have been laying out a funeral. I ran like one long stumble into his arms and buried my face deep in his belly. He could not make out what I was crying out to him. It was as if I was coming down the aisle to confess a sin and keep myself from the gates of hell.

My jaw beat against Packy's shoulder as he placed his hand against my back and locked me against his chest and made away with me. I felt like I was an imposter in a fortress that I did not deserve.

When we entered the preparation room, I did not want Packy to know what I had done. I knew he would know without me telling him, when he saw her. But she was gone.

Her mate was gone from the windowsill. When Moody entered out of breath behind us, I saw bits of gravel and tar staining on both his knees. There was some kind of leaf waving in his cowlick and I knew he had tumbled in his haste to help me.

Packy reasoned that one bird couldn't carry another. But if a bird could it would be the mourning dove, he said. The mourning dove mates for life and when one mate is gone, the other soon dies of grief or lives an empty life. Either way, I knew I had killed them both.

There would be no punishment for what I had done, at least not from Packy. And Packy knew that my punishment was my own pain and the searing heart that would reside in me for a long time to come.

***

Tara was bug-eyed all day and mumbling to herself and I knew she was balling up some kind of secret. A secret or something you ain't supposed to tell backs up in her like lava in a coffee can. She finally admitted to finding a piece of gnarled taffeta caught up in the barbed wire fence, back of her clothesline. I figured one of her kids put it there to scare their mama, which ain't funny no way. Probably it was one of her older boys.

It may have been Lancelot, or Hemingway. Could have been Rockefeller. She names her boys after people who are rich or have made something out of themselves, because somebody told her that kids are awful influenced by the name you give them. She has one boy whose first name is Doctor and his middle name is DeBakey.

She pulled the material sample out of what she calls the Twin Hills Bank, which is her brassiere, and told me it was pink, like the wild woman's dress. It was so worn and dull I couldn't say that it was pink, but I couldn't say it wasn't either. She looked at me as if I could say something to make her feel better, like *oh no this ain't the wild woman's*. But how in the world would I have known that?

Her anxiety made me feel badly for her because Lord knows I love Tara with all my heart. My favorite thing is to watch her ironing without her knowing. Sometimes she picks up something of mine and holds it in the air. She smiles or giggles and shakes her head while folding it tenderly. I know from that she is thinking of me.

I daydreamed about scratching on her boy's window screen at night to scare them back for her. Those boys scaring Tara just didn't seem right and it riled me up. I didn't want to scare Mozart though, because he is a bedwetter. But Tara never did nothing mean in her life, to nobody, to deserve being treated disrespectfully.

Tara had done a lot for me, and I wanted to do something for her. I owed something right back to the world anyway for what I had done to the mourning dove.

***

Nightfall was lazy in coming. The sun seemed to get stuck at the halfway mark as if it was taking an evening bath in orange sherbet clouds. The night shift began signs of coming on when the bugs started thumping against the front door screen and moths gathered to worship at the altar of the yellow front porch light. I usually started to settle a little downhearted when dusk set over me. But the trees were whisking their cool, calling airs in my window to tell me of their peaceful beauty in the night. The meadow smells were clean like mown grass with a touch of moldy trees, from their wise years of growing.

When the night calling overcame me, I shinnied down the jasmine trellis outside my window when I was sure I could hear Packy snoring deeply. There was a restful poise in the night air and it seemed all was well. Revenge on the boys for scaring my beloved Tara still seemed like the right thing to do. But when you are doing something that you don't have permission to do, there is a feeling inside as if you must successfully walk by a sleeping Goliath.

The dew in the air set my hair into a tight curl and weighed heavy on my chest. I ran for Tara's house so fast I felt I was lifting off the ground and my lungs began to pain me a little. The cool sweat that covered my body began to chill me, and I rasped at the air like I did when I had the croup in kindergarten.

Packy says a person makes mistakes when they go to doing something before thinking it all out. It dawned on me that I had not thought out what I was doing either. I had forgotten that noises in the night have a purpose, somewhere from which they come. The howls of distant coyotes were no longer distant, moving towards the stillness of the Sabine River. I frantically tried to remember if snakes slept at night or not. I knew coons stayed in their trees because that's how hunters kill them when they shine flashlights in their little halo eyes. If I was a Baptist, I could believe there were no such thing as ghosts.

When I was halfway between Tara's house and home, I began to wheeze from my running and the nippy air. My lungs were held back as if they were tied in a bundle like baled cotton.

I was ready to pass through a fringe of brush that runs the length of Parrish Carlisle's fence when I heard a swift passing sound and the trampling of leaves and underbrush. It stopped and started when I stopped or started.

I spotted a sugar pear tree that Moody helped me climb before. I ran for it as fast as I could and jumped at the lowest branch. A few excited wild dog chirps were close and a feeling crept over me as if I was in their sights. The low branch I grabbed at snapped like a wishbone. The ground met with me hard and the breath was knocked out of me, dazing me for a minute.

When I got back my wits, I reasoned that the old barn next to the pond was only two city blocks away. If I could make it there, I knew I could climb the corral posts next to it and jump up on top of it where the coyotes couldn't get at me.

Moody and I had been on the barn many times. We had a skateboard we fit in the grooves of the tin roof and we rode down the steep part of the roof onto the flat over the horse stables where we dug our tenny shoes in to stop. Twice Moody accidentally rode the skateboard on off the side.

If I couldn't make it, I hoped the coyotes would snap my neck quick so I would not see them tearing me apart. That would kill a rabbit instantly.

I was running like I weighed two hundred pounds and my spirit was giving up on me. There was not one angel in sight and I had no feeling like they were near. I knew they had forsaken me for a better little girl. The wild dogs could have me.

When my knees gave way and struck the path in front of me, I breathed in grit that set between my teeth and parched my throat. I curled up in a ball and prayed for Evangelise to hear my crying.

The coyotes began yelping faster and lunging shadows danced in the corners of my eyes. A galloping sound came from the side of me and I figured I was surrounded. I hunkered down farther to break the blow as the animal overtook me. Lifted at my belly, I was thrown over like a sack of potatoes and shaken with the movement of the creature. A warm umber glow was shimmering over the fence line like a shooting star, but I was moving so fast, I couldn't make it out. Then, I guess I fainted.

8

The Wild Woman

My face was warm on one side and I knew I was half dreaming. There was a balm over my eyes or something. I could make out the fire that was inside well-worn ground with limestone rocks encircling it. There was something moving behind it. The shadow had long scarf-like skirts and so much hair at the head you couldn't make out a face. It was dainty though. It was the figure from the night of the pirates but not so savage and scary now.

I blinked and batted to clear away the matter from my eyes to visualize the graceful soul. She came gingerly to me as if I was a rabbit she didn't want to run away. Offering me an old tin can with water for me to drink, I took it like it was proper. The matter melted from my eyes and I knew who she was when I saw the length of long red hair and the tattered sheaths of her lace-covered dress.

Through the flames and embers, she stood as quiet as a mouse in front of me. I was humbled that she had saved my life. It was clear the wild woman didn't bring me to her forest home to make chili out of me like Tara said she would.

I was treated with a velvety kindness and her movements were gentle so as not to frighten me. Her voice was a little shaky and squeaky from her solitude, but she made out alright.

The forest trees were her walls and their boughs were the ceiling of her earthy mansion. Her bedroom was a branch hut made of finely laced pecan limbs. They were protected with pieces of tin pierced and twisted with baling wire from the stacks of hay in nearby pastures. Just beside her home was a government water-testing well. It was a large round concrete cylinder with a small red windmill so the government helicopters could site it on rounds. The wild woman knew she would be safe and unseen there because the government never tends to their business.

When a stray cow or horse goes down in these parts the ranchers let their carcasses rot where they lay. You could watch a heifer go from a state of seemingly restful sleep to a molten web of rotted bones and fur. The buzzards and worms hasten the process and pretty soon all that is left are the chalky white bones and enough skin to make a wallet or maybe the sole of one moccasin. No one comes this far down into Wershepines for any reason, though they do not offer explanations as to why.

In her makeshift kitchen, the wild woman had some large bones to use as tools or perhaps a weapon if need be. There was a worn stump with a leg bone and some brown hulls where it looked like pecans were shelled out.

The china collection was an old pie plate and assorted tin cans and pots with half or no handles. She had an old Frigidaire with the door off and a sheet draped over it that I guessed was the pantry. She made good use of the litter that city folks had dumped in the country ditches.

The wild woman looked right pleased when I let her push the hair back from my eyes. She said she knew me a long time but I never saw her before. After so long of living in the wild, you must just sort of blend with your surroundings and become a fixture that belongs. She wanted to set the record straight and let me know the truth of her, and why she came to live in the lonesome woods.

The wild woman did not become some feral beast as Tara said, over the death of her beloved John Carlisle. And actually no one but Tara ever claimed sighting her, and she only said it to me and Moody. It was thought by the townspeople that when the wild woman heard the news of her beau's death, she donned her pink going-away dress, and walked through the woods straight to the Sabine River. From there she walked silently down the banks of the river all the way to Mexico where she lives today.

But of course, neither were true. She chose with a clear mind, to live around John's birthplace. In the world of nature instead of man, she felt she could be closer to his spirit. If not paradise in the beautiful meadow, her cursed lot would be to toil with matters of everyday life. He was in heaven, amongst the stars after all, and she would lay with him each night as she gazed into the same stars that surrounded him.

Parrish Carlisle got her nicknamed the Wild Woman of Borneo. He told other doctors and nurses about how his fine, pilot son had the nerve to court a midwife who once worked amongst headhunters and cannibals in the primitive forests of Borneo. There were hints and maybes in his tales about her, saying that the savages and the jungle rubbed off on her. He left out the part that she was there training nurses at an American missionary camp. He mocked her flowing red hair and thin frame, and love for being barefoot. He also left out the part of the story where she later came to work at a hospital near Clark Airfield in the Philippines. That is where she met the dashing young pilot, John Carlisle.

***

"It was Thanksgiving Eve when I arrived in Onward. Envisioning a warm welcome from my fiancé's father, instead what I got was Parrish Carlisle, in all his glory." She tilted her head back and squinted a little. She shrugged her shoulders and sighed.

"I can imagine a father wanting his son to marry a debutante from Dallas, as Parrish did. He didn't see someone raised as an orphan and a missionary nurse, fit for a daughter-in-law. But I couldn't fathom him using his political power to keep his son from taking leave from the Philippines, that was well earned, for the holidays."

She took a stick and made a circle in the dirt and tapped inside it before erasing it with her bare foot. She seemed to gather strength and went on talking.

Her gaze was upwards and slanted to the left as if she was watching a movie screen. "It was pure misery, staying with Parrish and his condescending smiles, trying to wait me out. He believed that I would fold under his pressure and stonewalling, from the discomfort of not being able to go forward with our Christmas wedding. But I was making my own plans, and looking for a small place for us on our own. And I had found one, in Onward, and was waiting for John to reply to my letters." She tapped the stick harder, until it broke. She began to pace.

"Then came the seventh of December. Parrish was shaken by the events of Pearl Harbor, but tried not to show it. He spent the majority of his time at his desk in complete and utter silence from the time of President Roosevelt's announcement of the attack until the knock on the front door, bearing the news of John's death. Ten hours after Pearl Harbor, Clark Airfield where John was stationed was attacked. Parrish began the bereavement of his decision to leave his son in harm's way for the worship of his own ego from the moment he heard of the Japanese invasion. He knew instantly that what he had done was wrong and he would pay dearly for it. And thus, his torment began." She quietened, and then took a breath and added, "He was already wounded by the death of John's mother for an illness no surgery could repair. And this just added fuel to the fire from which he was tortured within." She looked at me square then, and I nodded for her to keep talking.

"And it is true. I did put on my going-way dress, this dress." She touched the tattered hem and ran her fingers across the lace. "And I did walk to the Sabine River. But this is where I stayed. I could not bear to hear another word about John's death. I just wanted to be as close to him as I could."

"I did at times have vengeful thoughts in my mind of killing Parrish Carlisle for what he had done. But John shared his blood, and I could not do it, though I had many chances." She dusted her hands off and crossed her arms, replaying her thoughts.

"John had told me Parrish was deathly allergic to copperheads. That he almost died when he was young from a snake bite. He was playing near the kindling pile and he reached into the wood to hide a pocket knife his father had forbidden him to carry. The snake just came from between the logs, bit him on the forearm and recoiled back into its resting place. Parrish's whole body swelled and puffed up so you couldn't even tell who he was." She relaxed her arms and continued to pace.

"His fever got so high he went mad. He would have died if his father's nurse hadn't put eggs and sweet milk with sugar down a tube in his throat. His father just admitted him to the sanitarium for the mentally deranged, because he gave up on him. Parrish was strapped in a bed by all fours like a rabid dog. Every day the nurse fought him for hours until he wore down enough for her to pass a tube through his nose to his stomach and pour the mixture down it. He finally outlived the fever but his brain was affected like wiring messed up on electrical circuits. It must have burned up the part of the brain where compassion and mercy were housed because his mind never was the same." She turned back and put her foot up on the stump and rested her arms on her knee. After a moment's thought she continued a little more softly.

"I have seen a thousand copperheads during these years. I could have loosed one in his house and that would be the end. But each time I thought of it, I pushed it from my mind."

She sat down on a split barrel and log chair, rocking forward. Picking up a limb from the edge of the fire, she stirred the branches where it would burn better and the flames blazed higher.

"Should he have been afraid of you all these years then?" I asked her.

"Maybe." She admitted. "I have come close." Looking down, she didn't seem particularly proud.

"One time, I remember, I slipped in and turned the gas on while he slept. I saw him turn blue through the window in the early morning and I couldn't follow through. The fool." She lamented. "He has every opening secured except the floor of the fireplace. There is a metal plate that you push back on the floor of the fireplace to empty ashes into the ashbin. He never looked there because he never started the fire, even when the electricity was off during the ice storm and he was freezing. He has that chimney stuffed with paper and glass to light if I come down the chute."

"But why didn't I kill him?" she asked aloud. "I couldn't. I can't. It would be like killing a helpless child. I see John's eyes in his eyes." She paused a moment in sorrow, her mouth wrinkling a little.

She went to crying softly and I thought I might need to change the subject. The tears made clean tracks on the sides of her sooty, smudged cheeks.

By the light of the flames, I could see why people were scared of her. Her hair was matted and long and she was gangly like a skeleton. But there was still beauty coming off of her like she was a muse or a sweet innocent maiden. She was like a porcelain dolly you left outside in the sand pile.

"How do you get along out here? You look a might poor. Do you get enough to eat?" I asked her.

"Oh, plenty, child, yes I have plenty to eat. I have pecans, lots of pecans and roasted corn and plenty of sugar pears. I have barrels of them hidden and wild berries, persimmons, and possum grapes. I like to ferment possum grapes. Blackberries grow wild here too, you know. I grow potatoes and I get a few vegetables, now just a few, from my neighbors. I'm not greedy from other people's harvest. I always weed it or do something in return for what I take."

"What about meat like rabbit or squirrel?"

"No, I don't fancy them." She turned away innocently "I can't kill them."

"What about birds?"

"Can you kill a bird?"

She looked at me like a teacher that has asked you a smart question. You know you are going to get tripped up in the answer no matter what, but you will probably learn something. I remembered the mourning dove. My head dropped in shame and embarrassment.

"I have," I admitted. "But I won't ever do it again."

"One time?" she asked me.

"One time," I said. "And that was plenty to break me from that habit. I ain't ever been so sorry for something I have done."

"I, too, have killed one time, and given the same situation, I would do it again," she said defiantly. Her look of determination faded and she turned to me and smiled.

"But precious you haven't killed. Not really." She smiled playfully.

I didn't get what she meant.

She skipped over to her china cabinet Frigidaire like a two-year-old. She pulled back the sheet, and I saw she had put a window screen where the door was. Inside on a branch secured above the only shelf were the mourning doves. They cooed and fluttered when they saw her.

When I peered at them through the screen, I saw that the lady dove had only one leg. There was a poultice on the stump where her other leg had been that looked like melted purple crayon and cottage cheese. The wild woman had doctored her up with forest remedies and saved her life, like mine.

"When I grabbed her from the porcelain bed, she was slipping away. I brought her here and cauterized her stump with heated nails, which stimulated her some. It was enough to keep her breathing. Then I scraped the hull of green pecans and placed it on her tongue. The taste was so bitter she became excited enough to come to. She started fluttering her eyes, and turning her head. Her male companion just went crazy when she flapped her wings." She was smiling so widely, she could hardly speak and beamed at the love birds.

I knew it was a miracle, but everyone was safe. So, I didn't know why I was feeling stirred and hazy. Belliza slowly came into focus from the corner of my eye with her hands clasped at her chest and she looked like she was delighted and happy for me.

"Do you see that?" I asked the wild woman.

"What?" the wild woman said.

"Nothing." I answered, looking back in the Frigidaire. "They sure are a sight for sore eyes."

The wild woman and I visited with the mourning doves for quite a spell. And then something she said was picking at me, and I gently asked her a question.

"When you said you killed somebody before... why did you say you would do it again?"

She pondered for a moment and looked upwards again. Then she nodded to her thoughts and answered. "Do you know who the Fear-teller is?" She asked me.

"Oh, sure I do." I chuckled. "What child in Onward hasn't laid awake at night thinking about her?"

9

The Fear-teller

There once was a blind woman who could only make her way about in a wheelchair. This was not because her legs were paralyzed or her spine was broken. But because the sleeping minds of humanity were so burdensome to her core, that she felt boggy and overwhelmed with the weight of it. She was told by the angels that earth's inhabitants would eventually rise from slumber, but that the awakening would be slow, with a great deal of yawning and resettling before wilting eyes would finally be freed from the dream.

She was often seen reaching aimlessly upward in the air, thought to be searching for the hand of the Holy Spirit, to guide her from earth to a moment celestial. It was understood that she was among a few spiritualists extraordinaire for whom there was no opacity between love and fear, true and false, heaven and earth. She was one who stepped into the material world as an authentic essence.

The elder was often seen with an empty chair beside her speaking to it as if it held a wise and revered counselor. It was an exercise she employed when feeling that she was separated from her spiritual nature by some earthly conundrum. Presented in the chair was an illusion of herself at the age of seven when she felt she was the truest, the most earnest, making decisions only from the perspective of the overall good.

There was little focus on the bedraggled human vehicle she was blessed with, worn by the ego's tossing about. Portly and dimpled, she plucked thoughtfully at her frosty locks.

It had been said that two redbirds plucked her eyes from their sockets while she lay sleeping, and that she felt no pain. She had prayed for a new enlightenment about the ways of heaven and yearned to gain a higher level of learnedness to therefore grasp the workings of the universe. Her sight was sacrificed so that she could no longer see the façade of the material world, to be focused on all things eternal.

This new dispensation gave her a heightened sense of reality and a closer connection to those machinations we on earth cannot see or reckon with. It joined her with the divine world, where angels work diligently on their missions against forces in the earthly theater, to effect change in a struggle between good and evil.

From that moment, she could sense the undercurrent and the heaviness of fear and she knew when the layering of negative thoughts and emotions would give birth to an event or a happening in which the earth would suffer in harm, or death, or physical pain of some portion. When she became particularly stoic, some would hunker in their homes in silence until she was eased, and the calamity was meted out elsewhere. Known as a woman who could portend the brewing of worrisome occurrences and misfortunes, she was thereafter branded "the Fear-teller."

But ears are deaf to things which the mind is not ready to hear. And the wrath of man comes when he is threatened by his own ignorance. The Fear-teller had no audience or congregation to offer her wisdom. So therefore, she decided to join a traveling Pentecostal tent revival. In this venue, she was at least able to present her point of view.

As it goes with many tent revivals which are ultimately show biz with gimmicks like healing, snake-handling or speaking in tongues, she was a freak attraction. While the preacher condemned and barked about the sin of man to the townspeople, sweating and poking an open Bible, she was perched in her wheelchair on a side post offering a mystic or enlightened counter view. Though she was roundly booed and called a heretic, to the preacher's delight, she was at least able to plant her seeds in the garden of minds she would never have been able to harvest before.

And besides that, it paid the rent.

—Rev. C. J. Ellison, Tent Revivalist

The tent looked like a glowing square lightbulb in the distance. As the wild woman and I came closer, we heard beautiful organ music coming to a halt, and a voice being raised from a low murmuring sound, to then shouting. We came quietly around to the back side of the tent where the Black folks were congregated by a split in the tent that was partially pulled back. I noticed some of the fellas from the ice plant, and they smiled bigger than ever at me, and tipped their heads to the wild woman. They respectfully moved back so we could see. Not one person seemed afraid, and I heard one man say "Evenin', Charlotte."

Inside, Mr. Hubert was sitting quietly, almost prayerfully, on the organ bench with his hands folded and head down listening. He had beautiful caramel skin, a slender, rugged frame, and tight wavy hair. His eyes were amber gold, covered by little picture window glasses. Occasionally, when the preacher reached a high crescendo in his speech, Mr. Hubert would hit galloping chords. One leg sat motionless as the other popped methodically across the pedals. We could see in front of him the back of the Fear-teller's wheelchair with the handles, and her short, speckled curls.

The preacher challenged the congregants. "Now if you don't believe God abhors our wicked natures, you should turn your Bibles to Genesis chapter five and the story of Noah, who built the ark. This is where the passage tells us that God looked down on the creation of man with extreme regret, because of the sins being committed. For this sorry state of affairs, every mortal and beast were to be wiped from the face of the earth. God was ready to clean the slate." He held the open Bible far above his head and shook it. Then he placed it on the podium and paced the stage like a scheming badger, turning on his heel while he let his sermon soak in.

"But who was spared?" the preacher questioned them. He turned and pointed a finger towards them. "The one righteous man, Noah, who God instructed to build an ark! And he brought to the great boat, all who believed in God and two animals and beasts of every kind. These creatures presented themselves willingly to go within and be saved from the 40 days and 40 nights of flood, as God washed the earth clean of non-believers." He looked up to the sky and then down again, shaking his head.

"Can you imagine?" he bellowed. "How they beat their fists against the ark when water got about waist high!" He pounded his right fist as if against an imaginary barrier above him. Mr. Hubert followed his words with a hand over hand batting of the keys like he was swatting at a fly. He held the last low key down like he was killing it. Then he jerked his hands up quickly together, silencing the wheezy contraption.

The preacher was a balding, doughy man with brassy hair like men who brush Grecian formula through their graying spots. He turned to the Fear-teller to respond, smiling as if he had already dealt her a scorching blow. "What say ye to that, Fear-teller?"

She let go of her hair and rested her elbows on the chair. "Oh, nothing really. Because it is a chapter written in allegory. The meaning is spiritual. How could I disagree with the overall message that we get so far away from God and love that occasionally, we have to bring ourselves inside to our spirit? With that prayerful meditation, we wash away all the outward faults and material focuses to set our eyes again upon the Savior." She said it as if it was just common sense. The crowd was hushed, and they ruminated on that thought and the opposed views for a minute. Fear-teller leaned forward and peered with sightless sockets at the people.

"Because," she said, "Otherwise, if not allegory, we must believe that somehow two kangaroos jumped all the way from Australia, across the Indian Ocean to Turkey." She sat back with a thump to the back of her chair and looked strongly forward. She then shrugged her shoulders. "Not to mention, we would all be Hebrew."

The parishioners turned their eyes back on the preacher and gave a raucously mixed response of laughter, booing and shouts. Some loudly chanted, "Blasphemy!"

The preacher turned around smartly, his tie flipping against his rolled-up sleeves, and addressed the Fear-teller.

"You will someday beg like a fool for Lazarus to dip his finger in cool water to quench your parched tongue in hell." He turned his back on her and rallied the crowd to applaud him.

The crowd cheered and the preacher punched his fist triumphantly into the air. Mr. Hubert did not pepper this with chords from his organ and sat silently. The Fear-teller waited for a little quiet. Then her last statement was scarcely heard against the raised voices, as she answered him.

"Curious that you reference a passage that begins by saying, you may justify yourself before men, but God knows your heart." She unlocked her brakes and moved her chair back for a bit, preparing to leave.

The preacher turned fuming and snorting, while he bounced his eyebrows at Mr. Hubert, signaling that he should commence with the closing music. Mr. Hubert obliged with chords that sounded like a march. The preacher sauntered into the audience taking money and shaking hands as he slithered down the aisle.

When Mr. Hubert finished, he stood to help the Fear-teller navigate the creaky ramp to the floor behind the stage. The Fear-teller raised her head and looked into the air as if hearing a message, or having a vision, and I saw her kind face.

"Come," Charlotte told me. And we began our way back to the forest.

***

Charlotte held my hand as we started back to her homeplace. She seemed to be in deep thought. Finally, she cleared her throat and squeezed my hand. "You asked me how I killed without regret?"

"Yes."

"You know Mr. Hubert?"

"Yes, of course." I told her.

"Well one night, I was near here, and I heard a terrible crash and screeching wheels." She stopped for a moment, and surveyed behind us, pointing towards the road which we had just passed over. "When I got to the site, I saw an old white pickup truck, and they were hooting and hollering as they looked down below the bridge. Then they jumped back in the truck and drove away."

"In the gulley, hurled against the other side lay Mr. Hubert, barely conscious and moaning in pain. They had run him off the road. I started to go to him when I heard the truck in the distance, turning and coming back again."

Stopping for a moment, she sounded as if she wanted to reason with me. "I didn't know if they wanted to admire their handiwork or finish the job. They were racing their motor and driving furiously." She shook her head from side to side angrily. "I waited until they got closer to the bridge. You know where that marker is with the little bubbling natural spring and boulders are around the fountain."

"Yeah," I said. "Been there many a time."

"I stood in the middle of the road on the other side of it, and when they saw me, they floored the pedal." She straightened and stood tall. "I waited until they were close and then ran sideways for them to aim at me and jumped into the ditch, just in time for them to jam against the marker and the concrete pilons and boulders around it." Clapping her hands together loudly, I jumped.

"Two bodies flew through the windshield, against the structure and sprawled like scarecrows to the ground. Another one lying over the hood was engulfed as it burst into flames."

"I aimed to go back and tend to Mr. Hubert, but many people with the caravan of the Revival folks had pulled up and were jumping in the creek and starting the rescue. I had twisted my arm and couldn't move it without pain. I knew I would be no help to them. So, I went home and bound my arm and prayed he would survive."

"But why would they have wanted to hurt Mr. Hubert?" I questioned her.

"Oh, for terrible reasons," she said shaking her head. "Among them the foremost reason—that Mr. Hubert is Black. And also in their judgment, not fit to court outside his race."

"Mr. Hubert is Black?"

"Yes, his father was Black."

"Oh, I had no idea. And his mother?" I looked up to catch her eyes in the moonlight.

"The Fear-teller."

10

The Purple Heart

It is not always necessary to formally meet someone to have a bond with them. Perhaps while we sleep our spirits in communion go about the handiwork of forming what is to be played out in our conscious lives. Together, our souls pattern the circumstances that we are to walk through on the mornings after, like puppet masters in a play. Such is the foundation for feeling that sense of belonging or kin to someone the first time you lay eyes on them. Fellowshipping and witnessing the boundless ability of creative thought, perchance we struggle to whisper wisdom into our mortal ears. For our souls have one goal. And that is to make our short journey on earth one that will ultimately be worthy of the words repeated, well done.

—Rev. C. J. Ellison, Tent Revivalist

Charlotte and I could see the dying cinders of her campfire ahead as we neared her hideaway. She took my hand again as we were clearly in the darkest hour of the night.

"Those Black fellas were not afraid of you, because they know you, don't they?"

"Yes, all the Black folks in Wershepines know me." She did not seem to want to fib to me.

"Including Tara? Because I don't understand why she would tell those tales on you and want me to be afraid to come down to the Sabine." I stopped and put my hands on my hips. I needed some answers.

"Oh, she just wants to help me keep my privacy, she wants to protect me. She was probably afraid you would discover me." She walked forward and put her arm around me lovingly.

"Tara thinks if she keeps you terribly frightened it will override your curiosity of the Sabine River and possibly looking for me. She took a piece of my dress last week to try to convince you to stay out of the river bottom." Charlotte shook her head like she may never have believed in Tara's plan.

"Ha!" I laughed. "That is what brought me to Wershepines tonight, but for different reasons. I thought her boys had planted that material to frighten their mother. I was just going to get them back so they would have a taste of their own medicine. Then I got the scare of my lifetime. I have never been afraid at the river like I was last night."

"And the night of the motorcycle gang and that man they killed?"

"Yeah, and that night. I can't believe you weren't afraid to jump over their campfire." I said this with obvious admiration.

"It was nothing. I just saw what I thought was a flashing light. Maybe it was their fire, but I was drawn there. Something called me. When I saw you and Moody hiding, I knew I had to drive them off or they might take you."

It was deadly still when we made it back up the hill to her camp and I was tired. I rested by the fire and looked up at the stars. I wondered if John Carlisle could see me with Charlotte. With both of their spirits around me I felt safe, and then I fell into sleep.

In the early morning light, I awakened to Charlotte busily working around her place. She brought water and seeds to the mourning doves.

"You have to get home now, Cal." She said it with regret like she would miss me. "But I want you to have something. A gift from me, to always remember this night."

She half skipped over to the water testing well. Pulling up the thick, embedded metal valve, I saw a string dangling from it. On the end of it was a little oilcloth sack.

When she returned to me, she placed the purple heart with George Washington, our first president who never told a lie, on my chest. She stepped back and admired it with love.

"Wear this and know that I will always be here. And I will watch over and protect you as long as I live, Cal."

I cried. I cried a little at first, and it just kept growing until I was sobbing in her arms.

There is a kind of love that a woman can give. It is a kind of love that is soft, yet protective, and one that you know will never deceive you. One that only goodness will come from, and I had missed it so, for all my years.

***

Approaching the backside of our porch, I didn't need words to convince anyone of the circumstances of my night at the Sabine River Bottom, and meeting the real-life wild woman. As I came home down the path to our front porch, Moody looked like he had just gotten the good news he had waited for a lifetime. Tara held her breath until her eyes popped out like a sand crab. She fainted and hit the porch wood flat when she saw George Washington trimmed out in gold on the Purple Heart, bobbing on the collar of my shirt. Moody clapped his hands and jumped in place until he turned his ankle and flopped over on Tara. I stepped around them both and walked on in the house.

11

Parrish Carlisle

*There is a dark intensity, when looming, that can soak up and
swallow the air. It is not an angel or God. It is an invisible force that
overwhelms nature and the normal proceedings of the earth. When
you walk within the wall of it, you know that what is normal is not
what is unfolding. It is not a place where love dwells. The birds
do not flutter and fly about their business. They perch and station
in the trees. The cattle surrender themselves, perhaps in a place
where they are not usually found. There seem to be no bees buzzing
or rabbits running from one hiding place to another. Because all
spirits are connected, our hearts know when these times are upon
us and we act in the light of it. Though we know not the better path
forward, those of us who want to make things right press on and
walk through the shadowy circumstances without tribute to what
may come of us. That is the substance from which faith is born.*
—Rev. C. J. Ellison, Tent Revivalist

Packy taught me that there are many ways to take the Lord's
name in vain. You don't have to cuss. If you say you are no good,
you take the Lord's name in vain because when you speak of
yourself, you speak of God's creation. We are all God's kindred,
all parts of the Holy Spirit parceled out here on earth; the part
that can be seen with the naked eye.

I stopped looking at Moody like there was anything wrong
with him. I could not say there was something wrong with God.
When I studied him, I saw that he was happier than any human
I could ever know. Moody was blessed in that he had no place
for fear or saying something bad about somebody else. He loved
everything and everybody and he was just happy breathing. I
don't think he ever worried about money or where his next meal
was coming from, and each new moment in life held for him

one rapture after another. Living life without worry for what tomorrow might bring is a gift that few folks possess.

I was proud when Charlotte was anxious to meet him. It was an honor to go and fetch him to bring him to her. Sitting on the porch of his house was pure torture though, waiting for him to get himself ready. I could hear chairs overturning and water going on and off. He asked me if he should shave, and I said *I don't know; how long has it been since you shaved?* He said he had never shaved before.

When he came out the front door, my mouth fell open like a rusted tailgate. He had on brittle new blue jeans, a pearl-button cowboy shirt, brand-spanking-new boots and some kind of little ribbon on his chest. I couldn't say a word. Moody looked plumb handsome. "I been saving these clothes for a special occasion," he said. "This money came from selling my rifle and the Coke bottles I picked up since last summer." He looked at me shyly for a sign of approval, but my smile was growing so much wider, I think he knew I was pleased.

His sister, Jackie, was peering through the screen door when I asked him about his ribbon. "I won it." He said proudly. "I won the spelling bee."

I guess I looked a little shocked.

"Well, you looked surprised," Jackie said to me, sliding her head out of the door. "Let me guess, you thought Moody was a retard, right?"

"Don't, Jackie." Moody turned and looked hard at her.

"Well, he is not a retard, he is a savant. People get those mixed up." She stuck her tongue out at him as he tried to shush her. "He can spell and do math at high school level. Wants to be a physics professor. Will the excitement ever end?" she said mockingly.

"Don't listen to her, Cal. Let's go." Moody took my arm and guided me down the steps.

Together we made our way quickly across the fields toward the river. But the stillness of the Sabine made me wonder if it had suddenly gone dry. There was an air around like I felt the night of the coyotes, but I brushed it off thinking that night had somehow made me a fraidy cat.

Halfway down Wershepines Meadow, Moody picked up a Miller High Life bottle that looked like it was just thrown down. It was not yet dirty or the label worn light by the sun, and the last few drops spilled to the ground. It registered in my mind as something that wasn't right, but I went ahead on. There were tire tracks running around, several of them.

Sometimes teenagers get out and race their cars or park at night. Packy says they are smooching, which I think is taking other people's money without working for it.

Moody thought for a moment looking at the bottle. Then he turned to me and said, "I hope the pirates don't have Charlotte."

Moody was honing in on his intuition, and he breathed faster by the minute. I felt panic and worry that she was in danger too. Something inside us told us to move as quietly and quickly as we could.

When we came near to Charlotte's home for our visit, she was not waiting to happily greet us. In the distance we could see she was tied against the government windmill and her mouth was gagged. She had bright red blood in her hair that had run down into her eyebrows and her tattered dress was almost down to nothing but lining. She made wild movements trying to free herself, but she was powerless against her bonds. I knew that both of us should not go together.

I had to grab Moody by the seat of the pants to keep him from running to free her. I pulled him down in the tall thistle and milkweed.

"Listen, Moody. This might be a trap. We haven't seen the pirates leave and we know they've been here."

"But she's bleeding, Cal, I have to let her go." My finger was turning blue in his belt loop, pulling, as he was trying to stand up and run.

I looked at him desperately, but focused. "Yes, Moody, we must free her. But we know the pirates did this, and they may still be here. You have to stay here while I go for help." He nodded through his tears, but still looked like he was sizing everything up.

Moody raised his glasses and wiped a tear from his cheek with his shoulder and then positioned his glasses back in place to concentrate. "I hear you, Cal." He looked earnestly at me and I held him still by his hand.

"Alright then. I will be back as fast as I can, with help." He wiggled and looked like he was just going to take out running for her as soon as I let go of him.

"Moody, listen to me. If the pirates are around here and they see us, they will grab us and we will all be doomed. None of us will have a chance, including her. Stay right here."

He bit his tongue and looked from me to her. Bowing his head seriously, he nodded his head in agreement. "Hurry, Cal, you have to hurry so fast." His eyes were worried and he made me feel like he was depending on me.

When I started running, I felt like I would never get tired. Then I nearly stumbled when I heard a blood-curdling scream from Charlotte. Looking back over my shoulder, Moody was nowhere to be seen. *Darn him*, I said to myself.

I kept running blindly, but I couldn't think of where to go. Tara's house was almost as far away as mine, and sometimes she was late on her phone bill. I did not want to get to her house and not be able to use the phone, and I did not know if her neighbors had phones or not. I knew Tara's boys had guns for hunting to save money on meat, so if I could get all the way there, at least I could get help from them. Packy was most likely not home and I did not think I could carry his 12-gauge. It packed a powerful wallop even for Packy. He sported a bruise on his shoulder every time he fired it.

I thought because Parrish Carlisle was a doctor, a man, and somebody who could afford a phone that was always home,

I should hightail it for his house. His fence was also within distant sight.

Dr. Parrish had a two-story Colonial-looking house with black-framed windows and tall white columns. It reminded me of a mausoleum like the one where the Palmers laid Clovis Ray. Clovis Sr. and his wife could not see putting their baby into the ground. Like the mausoleum, Parrish's house had someone in it, but there was no sign of life.

All the paint was peeling on the house and vines grew right into the windows. Gray wood rotted around the casements and doors, and the water-stained trim flaked away. Sticky weeds and Johnson grass poked up through the pea gravel on his circular drive. The white picket fence gate lay on the ground barely attached at the bottom with a mangled hinge. The trees around the house had low branches and were leaning and smashed against it. The top of his pock-marked Cadillac sedan bore many tones of rust and fading paint. The flat tires were barely visible and tall, dry grass crowded the wheel wells. I recognized the small metal symbol on his back bumper that was the sign that he was a doctor. It had those snakes twisted around the rod. The edges were bent and it was raggedy like I figured he was.

I ran at his front door with full force. I hit the doorbell a hundred times but did not hear it chime or echo inside. I pounded on the door and screamed for my life. "Help, help, Dr. Parrish! It's me, Calvinia Jean Prather, Calvin Prather, the undertaker's granddaughter."

There was nothing but silence.

"I am not much more than four feet high and no more than fifty pounds soaking wet. I ain't going to hurt you sir. Please Dr. Parrish, I just want to use the phone to call the sheriff!"

I could hear stirring inside but not like he was trying to get to the door. More like he was getting situated until he waited out my leaving.

I hated to admit it, but I felt so desperate I started being a crybaby about it. In the back of my mind, the pirates had Moody and Charlotte strung up torturing them. I blinked hard because I couldn't stand it, and it emptied my eyes of tears. "I know you are in there, Dr. Parrish. If you don't help me the pirates are going to kill Charlotte." I sobbed it out.

That is when the stirring got a little louder. I heard paper tearing and the ripping of tape and I saw an eye look at me through the little tiny window in the door. The eyeball had a big white eyebrow with hairs about three inches long over it and he looked me up and down. He still didn't make any move to open the door. He pulled the cover back over the window and said nothing.

"Dr. Carlisle, this ain't a joke. Those motorcycle pirates have got Charlotte tied up to the government windmill and they probably have Moody too. You have got to help me!"

I guess he didn't get a good enough look because he went to pulling the paper and tape off the window next to the door. He looked me over again and tried to see all around me at the concrete porch, the bushes, and out in the yard. I could see he was thin and grubby. His hair looked like somebody had rubbed caramel in the white from all the nicotine of his cigarette smoking. He had a little stub of a cigarette smoldering in his mouth and had one eye shut to keep the fumes out. There were clean-shaven places on his face, but he had missed stray hairs at the corners of his mouth and under his bottom lip. As he held back the black plastic and paper, I could see he bolstered a 20-gauge shotgun on his hip. With his free hand he jerked the gun so hard and furiously he cocked it in midair.

"It's gonna be hard to talk on the phone with a mouth full of lead," he shouted back at me. His voice sounded like his tongue was too big for his mouth. It was kind of like Moody's mother late at night.

"Lord a mercy, Dr. Parrish. I don't want a mouth full of lead. There is no call to shoot me. Charlotte doesn't want to hurt you either. She has been caught up by those motorcycle pirates that killed that man down by the Sabine River. She doesn't mean you any harm." I pleaded with him.

"That will be the day, when Charlotte Perry means me no harm."

I swore that the grown-up man was pouting. I saw it as softening and I thought I might work it out of him.

"Listen here, Dr. Parrish. She could have killed you twenty times over. She doesn't want to."

"Like hell she doesn't want to. She can't get at me. You can't outsmart Ol' Parrish Carlisle." I did not know he was so prideful.

"Please, sir, let me in. She ain't with me. I promise on my grandaddy's life. If she wanted you dead you would already be dead."

"Bullshit!"

I thought to remind him of my age but times were desperate. "What if I prove to you she could get at you, Dr. Parrish? Would you believe me then?"

"What the hell are you talking about, little Prather?"

"Wait there a minute." I ran for the side of the house.

"Hey, where you going? Come back here. Don't you go around my house unless you want me to fill you full of lead. You hear me? Get yourself back up here, I'm warning you. You don't want your granddaddy putting you in a pine box, do you?"

I backed off from the house and saw that the chimney ran up from the roof where it must sit in the middle of the front room. I didn't know how I could get at the ashbin. It was hard to get to the cellar door through all the prickly barberries and the web of vines, but I tore at it furiously until I got an opening big enough to squeeze through, and it opened a few streams of light.

When I got inside the cellar it was just as I thought. The ashbin was situated next to the furnaces with an empty vat below it, maybe ten feet in. I climbed up on a wooden box and two old porch paint cans and placed a garbage can lid over the ashbin to get at the metal panel. Every time I moved the panel, old musty dirt fell in my eyes, and it took my breath. I shook it out of my hair and decided to get up on the lid, close my eyes, and stand and raise myself up.

As I lifted up the square on my head, it balanced until I got almost to my feet. I could look up enough to see the gloomy jail that Parrish Carlisle had surrounded himself with to keep off Charlotte. All the furniture was against the doors and windows with layers of garbage bags covering every window and door where no light was coming through. Even the rugs were rolled up and lodged against the doorways. Nails were fashioned into every window and some were bent at angles where he missed hitting them straight on, trying to nail the windows shut. The empty red wagon by the door looked sad, with the long rope that was Parrish's only lifeline to the outside world. He must have always kept it where he was ready to receive something, like a child waiting for a birthday present to come in the mail.

His back was to me with his head dipping like a fishing bob, up and down the window looking for me. "Ain't you allergic to copperheads?" I said to him.

He took the Lord's name in vain and dropped the shotgun on its butt when he whirled around. It landed on the cocked trigger and shot out a big piece of baseboard and plaster on the south wall when it fell. Silence fell over us as the dust settled and the plate clanged backwards off my head. He glared at me like he was paralyzed.

"Just play like I am a copperhead, one Charlotte could be setting loose on you right now. Or see me opening up the gas line in your bathroom while you are sleeping. I could kill you myself, Dr. Parrish. So could she."

Dr. Parrish picked the shotgun up off the floor. I thought to myself, if he really is nutty as a fruitcake, I might be meeting my maker. He turned the shotgun up on its end and put one knee up solid to be taller. The tip of the barrel went in his mouth and he started fishing around for the trigger.

"No, sir!" I said. I came out of my hole like an armadillo after a grub worm. I impolitely kicked the gun right out from under him and I heard it clang against his teeth.

"You have no right to kill yourself! You've got to make up for what you've done. Don't you see you can redeem yourself if you've got the courage and the gumption to be a man."

He slumped down and started to shake and cry so hard his body was pulsing.

"We've all got things we want to atone for," I said a little more compassionately, "I've got some myself." He cried more bitterly and buried his head in a folded arm.

"You can cry about it later," I finally said, losing my patience. "My best friend and my new friend, the one you've done wrong, need us. Where's the phone?"

"I don't have a damn phone. Who the hell would I talk to?"

I knew he was lying because I saw a fancy French phone on the corner table. But when I picked it up it was dead.

"Dagnab it all! I have wasted all this time here for nothing." I wanted to kick him and walk out but I knew that wasn't right.

"Why on earth did you let me squander all this time here? People's lives are at stake. And to think you are a doctor." I looked away in disgust and retreated to my hole in the fireplace and prepared to climb back down it.

"Wait," he said. "No, no, Calvinia. You haven't. Take me where she is. Let me help her. Let me help you."

"You sure that ain't just the sauce talking, Doctor?"

"I am sober from that now. You scared it out of me. Take me to her." He got to his feet and retrieved his gun. "Out the front," he said, and pulled it back with force, ripping away all the paper and duct tape.

As we ran out the front door together, Dr. Parrish grabbed a box of shotgun shells from a desk shoved against the front windows. For an old man he was spry, and I had to run my hardest to keep up with him. He squinted and shrunk back when the light hit him, but then he shook it off and went on as if the light of day was giving him the energy for the task we had at hand.

12

Evangelise

There were few times when Packy allowed anyone to drive the hearse. He fretted and worried so when the hearse was gone that he might as well have taken the time to drive whoever borrowed it, to and from where they were going. The hearse was always spic and span down to the air conditioning vents, which Packy detailed with Q-tips. When you work your fingers to the nub to buy something, you are likely to appreciate it.

Usually, he took Tara home in the afternoon, but he was waiting on a visit from a family to make arrangements for a loved one who was in bad shape at the hospital. Tara needed to get on home because her back hurt her something terrible.

She told Packy not to worry, that she wasn't pregnant. This type of low back pain she had never had before, never so intense and without periods of letting up. She said it was either a kidney stone or she had put her back out. With eleven boys she said she knew what birthing pains felt like. Finally, she looked to be so uncomfortable, Packy told her to take the hearse home and drive it back in the morning.

The doctor and I were making such good time my surroundings were passing by in a blur. I had my sights set on the trees surrounding the Sabine River and the opening where the windmill was nearby it, with signs that warned trespassers of the fine they would pay for going on government land. I didn't see Tara drive on the border of my vision on her way home. She must have thought the way we were hauling tail with that crazy-looking Parrish behind me waving that shotgun, that he was chasing me to kill me.

Parrish and I were headed straight for the windmill when I stopped still in my tracks. He knelt down, scared that I had seen something and pulled me to the ground. I was yanked so hard it nearly wrenched my leg off. I could see why he was not a pediatrician.

"What is it?" he demanded.

"Lord have mercy, Dr. Parrish, you nearly jerked a knot in me!"

"Why'd you stop?"

"I smell cigarettes."

"What? What the hell are you talking about?"

"I said I smell me some cigarettes. Charlotte doesn't smoke. Those pirates are around here."

"Get down!" he said and shoved me down again.

"Lordy, Dr. Parrish. Are you going to shove me in a varmint hole?"

"If I spot one. It is time for me to go forward and for you to stay right here. I don't want your blood on my hands." He stood up cautiously, looking over the meadow.

"Oh, don't you worry about me, Dr. Parrish," I said sincerely. I've got a guardian angel."

"That so?" he said sarcastically.

"Yep. She would be here right now but there is a shortage of angels you know."

"Great, thanks for telling me, Calvinia, but unfortunately there is no shortage of motorcycle thugs. So, you will watch for my signals and stop when I motion for you to stop and hide. If I get shot or captured, you will run to your grandfather for help."

"Oh, no, sir. My angel will help us out. She already did it the first time me and Moody saw the pirates, after they killed Mr. Leo."

"You knew they killed that man? You saw them?" He paused and shook his head downward, and dropped the rifle he held down at his thighs. "For God's sake, they are after you because you are a witness to it." He looked back at me with his forehead wrinkled.

"They are?"

"I can't believe I am here. I must be losing my mind." He pulled his rifle back up, cocked it.

"But, sir, you've long ago lost your mind. Everybody knows that."

"Thank you so much for your vote of confidence," he said with a fake little nod.

"You're welcome."

Parrish thought a minute and perused the landscape again. "Now those bastards must be in that gully over there because the wind is blowing from the east. That's why you smell their smoke. They are leaving Charlotte and your friend as bait to see if we take it. We will come up behind the gully. You will stop back by that hackberry tree and hide until I see what is transpiring. How many of them are there, would you say?"

"Well, I don't know for sure. There is one that is the boss named Red. He has more hair than a gorilla and wears a scarf like Aunt Jemima. You know, pirate-like." Parrish squinted harder.

"There is a bowlegged one with a long pigtail down his back and he is a might wiry. One of them looks young and stout, and then there is one with long hair that wears it down like a schoolgirl. He is tall as Packy."

"Damn. Four, maybe five of them."

"There were at least four sets of headlights when they hit the highway last time."

"Son of a bitch. This is too dangerous. You run right now, as fast as you can and get your grandfather. If they get me, hopefully your grandfather will have the sheriff here before they do us in. They are going to want to wait to catch you."

I crossed my fingers behind my back real tight and tried crossing my toes inside my tenny shoes. "Yessir. I'll go right now."

"Good," he said as if he was relieved. "I thought I was going to have to tan your hide." He patted me on the head like he almost had a soft spot. "Now get going."

I turned like I was going to run like the dickens. When I saw Parrish squat down, I slowed down and doubled back behind him. Parrish pulled himself through the weeds on his elbows. He weaved through the low spots like a snake, taking breaks when he came up behind a pecan or an oak tree. He wasn't like Moody. He steered clear of the Bois d'arcs.

I watched Parrish from a squatting position amidst the weeds and thistles. He angled off towards the pirates, and I crept up to hide behind the motorcycles. They were beside an El Camino with the back covered with a green tarp.

Closer to the gully I spotted the one with the pigtail and the stout young one. The young one had the blondest hair I ever saw with fair, blistered skin. They had rifles resting on top of the gully, pointing them towards the windmill. Red was sitting down in the gully smoking a cigarette pinched up on the end of a bobby pin.

Parrish stood up with his shotgun and aimed it dead at Red. "You hippy bastards, freeze!"

They went to shuffling like they were going to turn to shoot and Parrish shot the shotgun in the dirt beside Red and then cocked back the gun. That made them hold right where they were. He shoved a new shell right up under the shaft so they would know he was keeping the barrel loaded.

"When I say freeze, I mean freeze, sons of bitches. I would just as soon kill you."

They eyed him up and down and didn't move. "Now throw down the rifles first, then take your boots off and throw them in the gully too." The pirates hesitated a minute, Red got a smart look on his face with a surly grin.

I smelled sweat like somebody who doesn't take a bath. Before I could turn around, somebody picked me up by choking me under my chin and put a gun in front of my ear. Parrish turned to see me being carried by the scruff of my neck from behind the motorcycles.

"Drop it, old man, before I let Shirley Temple here have it," the Indian pirate said.

I don't look like Shirley Temple, I say to myself. *Shirley Temple is a sissy compared to me, going around singing lollipop songs.*

"Damn it to hell!" Dr. Parrish said at me. "Look what you've done!"

"That the one the retard was worried about?" the blond one said.

"Looks like her." Red was smiling like he won something. "And we got her granddaddy too. We need to go to Vegas. We are so lucky tonight!" He clapped his hands together with satisfaction.

I would have said that wasn't my granddaddy, but the pirate had my neck too tight. Parrish looked at me like I better pipe down. I thought this time I ought to mind him.

The pirates started tying Dr. Parrish and me up with rope, and Dr. Parrish went to cussing a blue streak until they duct taped his mouth. "Tie them against that hackberry tree until it gets dark," Red ordered.

"Let's do our business and get out of here, Red," the blond one said, like he was urging him.

"I'm the boss here. We wait until dark so we can finish with them. We can't leave out of here with four dead bodies in the light of day. What the hell is wrong with you? We leave at dusk."

"We are sitting ducks, Red."

"You heard what the retard said. Shirley here was going for her granddaddy and here he is. She'll probably tell us the truth anyway." He turned and looked at me. "You a good little Christian, Shirley?"

"Name's Cal."

"Oh, Cal is it? You a good little Christian, Cal?"

"I try to be."

"Is the sheriff coming? Did granddaddy here believe you and call the sheriff?"

"I tried calling, but the phone was dead," I told them truthfully. The pirates roared with laughter. Parrish rolled his eyes and shook his head real low.

"See, I told you Shirley here would tell us the truth. Our luck is holding out."

"How about the phone being dead, ha, ha, ha." The blond one reared back with laughter.

Red roared until he got it all out and then he became serious again. "We pull out at dusk. Get back in your places." The pirates snickered some and the blond one went back to his rifle.

"Time for some brews," the one with the pigtail said. He went and pulled the canvas back on the El Camino and brought them all back some Miller High Lifes.

When the Indian pirate strapped us to the tree, I saw that he had brick-colored skin. His hair was black as coal and he had not one hair on his face. He had a braided band on his head and I knew he was a real live Indian. He never once met me eye to eye.

Parrish looked at me like he hurt like a real person. He was scared and I could feel it. I told him everything would be fine and to trade out his fear for love. He looked wall-eyed at me like he did when I said I had a guardian angel.

When I think about love, I think about Mims and how she must have loved me. How it surely hurt her to leave me on earth with Packy. I know the angels didn't intervene because they knew that Packy would love me and care for me and I could make it without her and my mama. Maybe God needed Mims. No one could resist having her with them if they had the choice.

Thoughts about my Mims were taking over my head so that I thought I could hear her sing to me like she did when she rocked me to sleep at night. Packy said Mims was the only one who could settle me to sleep. And my mama had to get her sleep to finish high school. I was a colicky baby and I had a hard time sleeping through the night. Packy said she sang this song to me for hours. I closed my eyes and listened.

Calvinia, Calvinia.
I love Calvinia.
Calvinia, Calvinia.
Because she's so sweet.

I must have been going crazy. I could hear it like it was Mims herself, not Packy imitating her.

Calvinia, Calvinia.
I love Calvinia.
Calvinia, Calvinia.
Cause she's my girl.

Light was beginning to work its way through my eyelids because it was so bright.

The warm gold glow of Evangelise was heating me like I could feel her loving me. "Are you my Mims?" I said graciously.

Calvinia, Calvinia.
I love Calvinia.
Calvinia, Calvinia.
Cause she loves me.

"Oh, Mims! I knew it was you all the time," I said with glee and desperation all at once. "But right now, you've got to help us. This here's Parrish Carlisle and they are going to kill us both, and Moody with Charlotte. They are all set to kill us at dark!"

Evangelise had a sad look of pity on her face. "My darling, you know I would give you all my power and light, and I would tour again for you. But I haven't the light or the authority to deliver you. If I tried, I would only lose this time with you."

"That's okay, Mims," I said. "I'll get you some help."

"Clovis Ray!" I said as loud as I could without the pirates hearing me. Dr. Parrish squirmed. He must have thought I was losing my mind.

In a small white mist Clovis Ray came to us. He almost skidded into the hackberry tree. "Jiminy Calvinia! Oh, my goodness!" he said frantically. He looked at Evangelise for guidance.

"You know we haven't the power or the light, Asmin."

"I was afraid of that," I said. "I hate to do this... Maraeze! Belliza! And what's the other one's name, Mims? The bashful one that's light pink?"

"Enid."

"Right. Enid!"

I felt a coolness that made me shiver, but did nothing to Dr. Parrish. When the vapor cleared, Belliza had her hand over her mouth in anguish. Enid joined beside her in a meditative manor, and Maraeze had her eyes closed tight like she couldn't believe her eyes.

"Glory be," Belliza sputtered.

"Help me, Belliza," I said to her.

"Maraeze, what can we do?" Belliza begged her.

"Belliza. This is far too ominous for our intervention," Maraeze cautioned her. "This is an ill-omened moment and I know not what will come of it." I thought she was going to cry from her purple crescent eyes.

"We have to do something!" Enid said urgently.

"Evangelise!" Maraeze entreated.

"I am not advised, Maraeze. I have received no further instruction." Evangelise was humble and earnest in her talking.

"We have not the power together," Maraeze advised them. "This would take the light and height of a small legion of angels. The child can pray to the heavenly hosts to come to her aid, but I fear if she does not call them by name, it will not be of the amplitude to beckon them in time."

I hung my head, admitting to myself that fear was starting to win out over me. I had no other choice. No matter what came of me I had to do everything possible for Moody especially. I was responsible for him. He could never take care of himself. Maybe I still had something to make up for. I called in a hushed, throaty whisper, "Lucifer!"

"Oh no my child. You know not what this invokes!" It was the most excited I had ever seen Maraeze.

"Luuuuciiiiferrrrr!"

The pirates turned and looked for a moment but they turned back and kept on drinking their Miller High Lifes, thinking no one could hear me.

13

Lucifer

There is a concrete notion set in everyone. We are believers that we can work out every situation that arises if we call on our past to navigate the future. And when we get off on this self-directed course of our own thinking, we simply spin our wheels and delay our mission. These diversions from our highest good are born from our past fears and are a knee jerk reaction to the material world passing before our eyes. What can save us is the hand and the inner voice of the Holy Spirit. When we lay the Holy Spirit's hand aside, we detour from a smoothly paved road onto one that is littered with thorns and stubble. We might as well drive cars with wooden windshields when we draw from our past instead of leaning on a holy, omniscient being. Why keep the wheel and not surrender it when there is someone beside us that can actually see the road ahead?
—Rev. C. J. Ellison, Tent Revivalist

When I opened my eyes again, I could only open them for a second and then look away. I was overcome with the brightness so much that I felt my eyeballs were going to burst.

"Don't look directly on me, child," said the mighty Lucifer.

I could see that Maraeze, Enid, Belliza, and my Evangelise had all gathered together in a huddle surrounding Clovis Ray. Evangelise knelt with her back to Lucifer; the others were shielding themselves with their wings of light over their eyes. I knew Evangelise had not been an angel long enough to have the tiny hand-like wings.

"For what do you beckon me, child." His voice echoed like Zeus' did on the Hercules cartoons. It was deep and had a rumble to it like thunder.

I could see Clovis Ray was squinting and trying to see out from around Belliza's round body. He was shaken and scared.

"Well, I don't know where to start, sir," I said to him honestly.

"I am aware of your circumstances, child. For what do you beckon me I say?"

"Sir, I know you have the power and the light to help me. My best friend, Moody, and a woman who has been alone all her life until now, and me, and Dr. Carlisle here are about to meet with death. Now I don't know how this works. I know in my heart I am going to be an angel because I'm a special purpose child."

"And?"

"I will do anything you ask me to if you save these people's lives. I'm a hard worker, though I am not straight A because of math. I can read two levels above my grade. I can do my share of chores and the next fella's too."

"You want to be of service to me. You are willing to join my angelic order?"

"Well, sir, I don't know that it is my first choice, but I do want to save my friends and do what's right by them."

"Huh," he chuckled. "You have called Lucifer to these parts of Texas to save the lives of these people? This is most amusing." He laughed again.

"Yessir, that's it in a nutshell."

"I tell you then. If these three angels together, Maraeze, Belliza, and Enid, will agree to another tour and I take Asmin, I will solve this small problem for you."

"No!" cried Maraeze as she pulled Clovis Ray back inside the huddle.

"Sir, I was more offering myself. And what about these here pirate fellas? You sure you don't want to take them with you on your way? I know there's a shortage of angels."

"Child, these men are not of angels. They will not have wings at their death. They are useless to me. You see, my child, the problem is not so much that there is a shortage of angels in the heavens; there is a shortage of angels on the earth."

"Oh." I guessed he was right. There would not be problems like we have here on earth if we all lived in love like the angels.

Lucifer paused for a moment and said, "As for you, I would take you if it was your heart's desire. But I would never take you if you do not understand what I would have you to aspire to do with your light."

Maraeze clasped Clovis Ray's mouth as he continued in protest.

"Now I will be off, child. You have taken much of my time. Until you have something to offer me in exchange, for what would I give you light?"

I was desperate and I thought if he left that my chances of saving my loved ones were gone. "No, sir, don't go!" I said. "I promise you, I have changed my ways before and I can change my way of thinking again!" He turned back with a slight trace of interest.

"Really?"

"Yessir. I have things I want to atone for. If I hadn't gone to the Sabine River Bottom like Tara told me not to in the first place, none of us would be here."

"You don't believe this was all just according to the plan?"

"I believe the plan could have been different if I never did something I shouldn't have in the first place. I didn't do what was right, and here we are."

"You are a strong believer in doing what is right?"

"Yessir, I am."

"Then how will you come with me after all it is you believe."

"Because right now I owe it to these folks, and I believe that this is the right thing for me to do. I believe it with all my heart."

"But you must understand the order of things, my child. You realize you must transform in order to come with me?"

"Transform?"

"Your earthly body must die for your soul to be released as a spirit being."

"Well, I guess that goes without saying." I looked down, hesitating only for a moment. "You could make it quick?"

"In an instant."

"Then I understand, sir, and I am willing." I said it with as much meaning as I could.

"Very well then, I will take you and Asmin." Lucifer looked pleased at his negotiations. "And the seraphims will take another tour!" He laughed maniacally and lifted his chin toward heaven.

"You will not take these children!" Maraeze screamed with anger as her light began to swirl around her. Enid and Belliza aligned beside her and they all surged forward towards Lucifer as if they were trying to fend off his light and mount a force against him.

Evangelise grabbed Clovis Ray and turned him with her and put her arm around him, shielding him from the brilliant light and mounting winds.

Maraeze and the others were suspended in the air as they struggled with their arms and their wings against Lucifer's force of light. He smiled and chortled and toyed with them and the air around them as they thrashed and turned in their battle. Belliza was beginning to cry out in agony from the force and the loss of her energy.

The struggling angels seemed to break through and tried to soar headlong at Lucifer, when a great wind came upon them and they were caught up in the draft like the eye of a tornado. They were tossed about and their auras began to desert them as colorful flares flowed to Lucifer. They were caged inside the eye of the storm and became a freefalling merry-go-round towards the earth. A large band of light came forward from Lucifer like a spear and pierced the meadow. When they came to the ground the soil parted and the warm glowing light beneath it swallowed them up like the last bit of water going down a drain.

I shuddered to see them leave. Clovis Ray came nearer and hovered over the tree where we were tied. Evangelise went into a state of meditation so as not to be caught up as Maraeze and the others had been, and she was silent. I covered my eyes and tried to squint in such a fashion that I could look on Lucifer. He was in a trance-like state and beams of amber, orange, and red streamed about him.

The earthly silence was broken by the sound of a racing motor. As I looked out across the field, I could see a cloud of smoke behind Packy's hearse. The long black Cadillac hearse jumped and dipped so on the meadow bumps I could tell it was going at a furious speed.

The pirates turned and stood like statues and gawked at it at first. The hearse passed between us and the pirates and I saw the helmet shape of Tara's hair as she flew into the line of motorcycles. The cycles were pushed aside and smashed like a sandwich between the hearse and the El Camino. All the while Tara screamed, "Help me, Lord, help me, Jesus," like she did when she was in church or right before she started an episode of speaking in tongues.

Oh no! I thought. Not Packy's prized hearse!

The pirates began to scuttle to the car and held their guns on her. "Bitch, get out of the damn car!" Red screamed at her.

I could see Hemingway, Lancelot, and Einstein creeping over the side of the gully when the pirates turned their attention on Tara. With their rifles cocked they took aim at the pirates.

"Don't call my mama a bitch!" Hemingway said.

"Drop your guns!" yelled Einstein.

The pirates turned as if they were going to resist the order as the hearse doors flung open and Rockefeller and Hank Aaron perched their guns on the ledge of the wide door.

"Drop 'em like my brother said," Rockefeller ordered again. "Or me and my brothers will shoot your legs out from under you."

The pirates dropped their guns in the dirt to surrender. Doctor DeBakey and Edison came from the woods behind us and began to loosen our bonds. Doctor DeBakey was leery of Dr. Carlisle and loosened his ropes standing back from him as he marveled to see the legendary hermit he had always heard about.

Over the edge of the gully came Moody first, rubbing his wrists. He looked stunned like he had been through something he did not understand or could not believe. He smiled when he saw Tara's familiar face like all was well again and began to trot to her for safety.

Charlotte crept cautiously over the side of the gully until she could make out the situation. When she looked convinced that Tara and her boys were in control, she relaxed a little but kept her sights open. Livingston followed her, folding up the pocketknife he had freed them with.

My heart filled with joy as I saw Packy's black Cadillac coming across the pasture. I saw the beautiful black little heads of Pharaoh and Mozart in the passenger's seat, whom I guessed had run to get Packy.

"You all right, Mama?" Hemingway asked as he opened Tara's door to retrieve her. She was moaning and groaning and holding her back.

I hugged Lancelot around his waist when I came around the car, and he handed his gun to Dr. Parrish so he could hug me back. Dr. Parrish moved close to the pirates like he had no trust for them. Lancelot and Rockefeller began to gather the pirates' rifles and search their pockets for other weapons.

Then we were all startled by a sound that was like someone throwing out a pail of water. Just as Hemingway retrieved his mother from the car a gush of water coursed down her legs and made a large puddle beneath her. "OH NO!" all the boys cried out together.

Tara closed her eyes like she could not believe it and slowly shook her head. In an instant during the excitement of it, Red bent down quickly to remove a pistol from his boot.

Without hesitation Parrish Carlisle emptied a shot from his shotgun into Red's chest from where he held the rifle at his hip. The sound of a quick wisp of air mixed with pain pressed from Red's lips. He turned and swiveled with the pistol in his hand. He weakly squeezed off one round as he fell to the ground.

My world turned from a feeling of realness to one like I was viewing a slow-motion movie screen. A ghost of a light gray man emerged from the body of Red and walked steadily upward without telling us goodbye, kiss me where the sun don't shine, or anything.

I felt an easing in my muscles and my body folded up like a church fan. My face was in the dirt but I could not turn myself over.

14

The Calling

Fear was not created by God. Because God gave us the power to reason and create for ourselves, we prescribed the birth of fear. But the only substances that are real and eternal are those that are born of love. We all come from love and it is that to which we will someday reunite, no matter what. We may choose to return to it even while we are here on earth. It should be known that the Rapture is not a one-time event; it is something that takes place every day for those who claim it.
—Rev. C. J. Ellison, Tent Revivalist

I can't say that I was in pain or hurting. But there was a hard stillness that showed me that I was no longer in control of the goings on of my body. Taken by a sweet love for sleep, my body yearned for rest. Calmness was so overwhelming that I had no reaction, even for the warm blood making a puddle around me. Voices and sounds were fading as if I was slowly turning down the volume on the television.

For a moment, I was startled to turn back and wake up my senses when I heard Packy crying out, "Cal, Cal! My baby Cal! Gracious God, do not take my baby now! Cal, don't go. Can you hear Packy? I love you, baby. Packy loves you."

I thought I was raising up to comfort him. But as I sat up my body stayed behind. When I got my bearings, I realized I had little wings like Clovis Ray. I fluttered them a bit and looked around for Evangelise. Praying hard, she was not looking at Packy or me, being earnestly set in her meditation.

Lucifer continued with his spells and incantations as different shades of red were shooting ever' which-away. He motioned and contorted himself like he was conducting the climax of a symphony chorus.

Another gleaming white angel had joined Evangelise. I wished they were here for me, but I hadn't lost control of my senses so that I didn't remember my soul belonged to Lucifer.

From a lofty height above the trees, I looked down on Packy, Tara, Moody, and the others. Dr. Parrish had Moody pressing hard on my upper leg where the blood was coming out, while Packy held my feet up. Charlotte puffed breath into my mouth as Dr. Carlisle pushed my chest up and down.

Some of Tara's boys had the pirates on their bellies with guns to their heads. Their arms were shaking with anger, and they looked like they wanted any little reason to pull the triggers.

Hemingway and Lancelot rushed to load their mama into the back of the hearse. It was such a sturdy tank it had few marks from the crash. A trickle of warmth fell over me when I realized the angel that had joined Evangelise was the white angel that I knew to be Fanny J. Crosby. I met with bittersweet thoughts to be honored with her coming, yet shameful that it was not a joyous event.

Thinking back on the moment that I spent with Rosemary brought soothing memories to me. My heart was sad and heavy as I went on to singing the song I sang when I first met the great Fanny.

Pass me not,
O gentle Savior,
Hear my humble cry;
While on others thou
art calling,
Do not pass me by

Fanny lifted her head and lightly smiled, beaming with triumph. She sang softly with me.

I wanted to keep my eyes on Packy, in case I wouldn't see him again. But they jumped back to the ruckus with the rise in the campaign of light and conjuration of Lucifer. The skies of the earth began to change, though the people on earth did not seem to notice. There was no lightning, but there were mighty rolls of thunder.

"No!" Lucifer cried out. He came towards me with a face of fury so filled with rage he looked to be wholly desperate. The clouds began to billow and wave, moving apart as the sun came streaming through in a long golden ray. My eyes could not look directly on it, but I could see Lucifer fully as his light had paled. He was a dog-faced lion of a man, with more claws than fingers.

"She has given her oath!" Lucifer declared against the overwhelming radiance. "She is promised to me. I have given of my illumination to her. This is not just!"

Clovis Ray had moved over to Fanny. They were kneeling all the way down as if they were lying on the ground, though they were high above the trees. Their robes were snapping in the fury of the winds from the heavens. As the beams parted the clouds, the glare became so bright I had to shade my eyes to still see them.

There were thousands of angels behind the clouds. They were all of the brightest white and a brilliance that I could only imagine coming from the Great I Am.

"The Great I Am cometh!" Fanny J. Crosby called. "Bow yourself and shield your eyes, my child!

I could no longer look at the magnificence coming from the heavens. My hand did not cover enough to take away the blinding shine of the light and I had to turn away.

Lucifer cursed me. "Damn you, Calvinia Jean Prather. You sing praises to your Savior even while you have promised your soul to me. You have defiled your word and dishonored your angelic oath! The vow is broken and you shall pay dearly!"

Lucifer no longer directed himself towards me. He turned himself towards earth and began to send scorching beams of lightning down on the pirates.

The great golden storm ricocheted back against Lucifer as he shielded his own eyes and screamed in anguish. He cowered for a moment in the wake.

"I will give no more light to this, Calvinia Jean Prather! You will pay for this lie and this treachery!" He was getting more sore with me by the minute.

"The child has dealt no treachery or mischief, Lucifer," came a voice from the front of the heavenly beings. "The child has merely bid her Savior not to pass her by, and her Savior is here."

"And so it shall be!" Lucifer spat. "I will not take this child who has no respect for her word. I have no use for her and her stealing of my power and light. I leave you, Calvinia Jean Prather. Never utter the name of Lucifer from your mouth again!"

Lucifer's radiance could still be seen for moments after he had departed. It died out slowly with the mighty power he still retained.

The heavenly hosts were silent in their honor and worship of the Great I Am. From the shielded corner of my eye, I could see that they turned to bow. They covered their eyes with their wings of light and kneeled in unison. I could not look upon the Great I Am, though my heart was hungry to see.

"Thank you," I said. "I don't know how to thank you, but I love you with all my heart."

The great burning band recoiled victoriously back up into the clouds. The surrounding sky began to close like great mansion gates. I could open my eyes fully again.

Fanny and Clovis Ray got to their feet. She called to me with an outstretched hand, and I knew it was time for me to go with her. I looked back at my little wings and fluttered them. They lifted me and I saw flying was going to come natural to me. I began to make my way towards Fanny and Clovis Ray.

Evangelise continued in her fervent prayer. She did not change or flinch with what was happening around her.

"Come on, Calvinia!" Dr. Parrish cried as he continued to push on my chest. "Come on, Cal! I know you have it in you. You can do it, Cal." He stopped a minute and put his head down on my chest, and felt for the pulse in my neck. "Let me breathe her a minute," he said to Charlotte.

He started pumping harder, like a mad man. Faster than the rhythm he set before and he took deep breaths and pushed them quickly into my little earthly body.

"We need some help!" Hemingway called from the hearse. We need somebody to help Mama."

"I'll go with you. I have birthed a hundred babies in Borneo," Charlotte offered. She jumped up in the back of the hearse with Tara. "Please help her, Parrish!" She screamed back at Dr. Carlisle. "I will go, but don't give up on her. Keep trying!"

I hovered looking longingly at Packy. "I guess it is time to go," I said to Fanny, holding her hand.

"When Evangelise is directed," she answered me.

Evangelise raised her face up from her prayer. "To God be the glory," she said.

She came over and floated with us for a moment. I felt her warmth and her love like only a mother or God could love a child. Her smile was calm like all was well. She reached out her hand for me and I felt consumed with her spirit. I smelled Mims' perfume again, and I had visions of her on earth, holding me as a toddler.

I slowly began to lower towards the earth as Mims and Fanny squeezed for the last grasp of my hand. I felt like something was vacuuming me up. My senses blurred and I was sleepier than I was before, and then I guess I fell to earth. I could hear the voices becoming louder and higher.

"All right now, we have a beat. Let's get her in the back seat of the Cadillac. Mr. Prather, you drive and I will tend her in the back. Let's go!"

My body was lifted into Packy's car. Moody never once lost his grip on holding Packy's handkerchief over the bend of my leg where Red shot me.

Hank Aaron, Lancelot, and Livingston were picking up the pirates who were bound up like sausage links and loading them into the back of their own El Camino, where our bodies were to be laid.

My senses left me again and I fell into deeper sleep. I could hear Packy as I drifted off. "Packy's got you, Cal. Packy is driving you to the hospital so they can take care of you, sweetheart. Packy is here." Then he cried like a baby, "Don't be scared."

15

The Special Purpose

When a little one is hurt or wronged it is a mortal sin, which makes everybody pause. Doctors and nurses are shaken to the core when bearing witness to the tragedy of injured children. Great knowledge and steadiness are required of them, without regard to the tightening vise around their own hearts.

There is a sweet innocence in children that is as meek as a baby fawn. They are trusting, vulnerable creatures that wear their hearts like a delicate suit of clothing, as tender as the skin of magnolia petals. When someone harms a child that someone becomes lesser, because they must live with a soul that has been betrayed.

—Rev. C. J. Ellison, Tent Revivalist

When we arrived at Onward Memorial Hospital, we needed no introductions. After twenty-odd years of hiding out, the staff knew Dr. Parrish Carlisle had not come in to have coffee and chat. They took his orders like he had been there all the time and wasted no time getting me to surgery.

As the news of what happened spread through the town, people fought to get in line and donate their blood. Mr. Hubert balanced on a cane, with his head down in serious thought. He folded and unfolded the papers for his donation as he nervously waited. He looked worried that they might reject him. Maybe they would not want blood from his kind.

Packy stepped out of the line of shaking hands with people and approached the nurses who were preparing the donors for their offerings. He took Mr. Hubert by the elbow and then placed his arm around him. He brought him before the nurse in charge.

"Francis, take this gentleman next," he said. The nurse looked a little puzzled, and Mr. Hubert bowed his head and raised his shoulders. A little tear streamed from his eye. "There will be no closer match." Packy nodded and patted Mr. Hubert's back sincerely.

"When they finish with you, come stand with me at the waiting room, please," Packy invited him. Mr. Hubert gushed a little crying sound with more tears, and nodded without saying a word.

Prayer circles were scattered from the front lobby to the ambulance dock, asking God for mercy to save my life. Folks got on their knees that had not been on their knees for some years. They stopped lobbying God for their own needs and asked for me to cut to the head of the line.

Old wounds healed without scars and grudges disappeared like the unlikely Texas snows in March or April. Like snow and ice, people melted off the cold and hardness of their hearts to a cool water that nourishes the earth and all its beauty.

The nurses and orderlies put me on an operating table that practically stood me on my head while they poured precious blood into my veins. They wrapped Dr. Carlisle up in all kinds of dresses and hats so that only his piercing eyes were showing. Instruments were unwrapped and ready as the nurses remembered without being told his glove size and the instruments he favored using the most.

He went about patching the artery in the top of my leg like Packy would make a pot of morning coffee. It was simple for a gifted surgeon like Dr. Parrish, and he commanded it like it was the reason for which he was born.

When Dr. Parrish called for another medicine to be pushed or dripped through my veins, the nurses were already holding it as if they were waiting for the signal. If he hadn't thought of it right off, they would act like it was his idea and say things like, "I have the epinephrine ready, Dr. Carlisle."

It was amazing to float around, near my body, watching so many people show how much love they had for me. If I live, I will slam a door on my hand before I ever say a cross or angry word to any one of them again, for the rest of my life.

Packy nearly wore the soles off of his boots pacing the surgical waiting room.

Moody ran from labor and delivery back and forth to keep Packy informed about Tara. "It's a girl!" Moody said on one final arrival.

"*A girl!*" Packy said in amazement. "I hope that means this is a day for miracles! Eleven boys and Tara has a girl!"

Tara's boys erupted in disbelief. Mozart asked Hemingway if he wanted a glass of water. "You lookin' pale," he told him.

"What about Cal?" Moody asked Packy carefully, hoping there wasn't bad news.

"We don't know yet, Moody."

"I'll check Tara again," Moody said and was back off down the hall. Ten minutes later he returned.

"It's a girl!" he said to Packy and all the others waiting.

"I heard you the first time, Moody."

"No, Mr. Prather. She got another girl."

"Lord have mercy!"

Tara's boys erupted again and Hemingway's knees got shaky. "Sit him down." Packy directed. "Mozart, did you get him some water?"

Jewel Ellison, Moody's mother, pushed through the door as sober as a judge. "Moody!" she pleaded. She grabbed him like he was a soldier who had come home from war, and pulled her fingers through his patchy hair. She kissed him all over the face like he was something special and he turned as red as a fire ant.

"I've got to go check on Tara!" he said to his mother. She let him go and slumped down in a chair to cry her eyes out. When his sister, Jackie, came in, she cried too, no matter how mean she always was to Moody.

"It's a girl!" Moody announced it again as he skidded back in the door.

"Moody, for the last time, we know Tara has two girls," Packy said like a parent.

"No, Mr. Prather, three girls. Tara has got three girls."

"Son of a gun!" Packy said. He slapped his leg in amazement.

Tara's boys began playfully shoving each other and howling with laughter. This time Hemingway went to the floor with a thud. "Put his legs up, put his legs up!" Packy directed them. Mozart drank the cup of water himself, over Hemingway, and slowly shook his head.

My soul felt a warm presence and I could smell the spicy gardenia of Mims' perfume. I saw her glow and she came sweetly to me. "Come sit with me." She offered me her hand and lifted my spirit with her to the rooftop. We sat on the shingles and hung our legs down looking into the operating room and watched them get me ready to move out of surgery.

"I want to tell you some things while we have these last moments together. This mission will work itself out for a long time to come. But when you awake, you won't remember all that has happened. Though I am still your guardian, you won't remember me unless we are called to meet again."

"What?" I said with disappointment. I didn't understand.

"Think of all you have witnessed, Cal. You will need to carry on a more normal life again. But I want to tell things to you now so you will have an easier time understanding them, when you are faced with them soon." She looked at me intently, like there was no choice in what was best for me.

"Okay," I said, trying to be reasonable and respectful. I wanted to hear anything she had to say. "Tell me."

"I want you to know that your mother and I were killed after we were run off the road. We were in the car with your father. He was thrown free to the bank of the stream, but your mother and I were trapped and unconscious and we drowned."

"But wait, Mims, I have wanted to ask you where my mother is. Why hasn't she been with you? I mean isn't she an angel too?"

This had been eating at me for some time; that I was able to see Mims, but not my mother. I thought maybe she could call her.

"No, Cal. Your mother was a beautiful young soul. But she rose into heaven as a spirit and that is how she remains." Mims looked me in the eye and waited for me to understand it, without speaking further.

"But Mims, you are an angel. And I was an angel for a minute there. If she is your daughter, and I am your granddaughter, how is she not an angel?" Not only did this not make sense, but it just didn't seem fair.

"You don't just have me, Cal. You have your other grandmother, from whom you also inherited your abilities."

"My other grandmother?"

"Mary Catherine Hubert."

"Mary Catherine Hubert?" I said dumbfounded. My mind was reeling. I kept searching her face for the answers.

"You know her, Cal. You just know her better by what she is called. The Fear-teller."

I slumped down. It was all coming at me so fast. I couldn't put all the pieces together so quickly.

Mims and I floated with my body to the area where they moved me to recover. Leaning with his back against the wall, with his hands behind his glasses, Mr. Hubert had tears leaking between his fingers.

Dr. Carlisle told Packy I was not out of the woods, but he had high hopes I would make a full recovery. What Packy said after that, nobody knows because he was crying so hard with tears of joy. He patted Mr. Hubert on the shoulder and they both wiped tears from their eyes with their handkerchiefs.

Packy was allowed to hold my hand while I lay sleeping. He looked apologetically at Mr. Hubert. "I'm sorry, Terence." Packy was speaking sincerely.

"No, Mr. Prather, this is right. It will take time." He nodded at Packy with smiling tears.

My heart felt like it was swelling, and I did not know fully what to make of everything. "Does this mean?" I turned to Mims, still a little bewildered.

"No, Cal, please don't worry." Mims laughed. "You do not have to learn piano."

***

When I was little, Packy would take a fallen eyelash from my cheek and hold it between his fingers. He would tell me to make a wish and blow it free. I always wished for whatever I didn't have at the moment like candy, a million dollars, or a driver's license. But when I got older, I always made the same wish. And that was for my soul to grasp the hand of the Holy Spirit to lead me to the miracles for which I came to earth to uncover.

Miracles cannot be conjured or created by the conscious mind. They are moments crafted through spirit that afford us a short release from doubts and fears. In that moment our eyes are awake to what matters and petty things of our previous focus, dissolve to nothingness. There is no more rapturous moment than the freedom bestowed by the unfettered love and hope we feel when a miracle is coming to pass.

And the miracle of my life began on that day when I was delivered from my mortal wounds at Onward General Hospital. There began my solemn devotion to bring love and human understanding to the world around me. And as the Baptist would say, I surrendered to preach.

It was with great joy in later years that I joined my father and grandmother to form our own traveling tent revival. And I had no bigger fan than one front row regular, my Tara, with tambourine in hand.

I would like to think she was there mostly for me and my beloved Moody. But with tender jealousy, I knew she reveled more to see how the crowd loved to hear the angelic voices of her three daughters. I suspect they could even draw the crowds alone. Baptized with names that came to Tara in a dream, the amazing voices of daughters Maraeze, Enid, and the soul-shaking contralto Belizza, were... heavenly.

—Rev. C. J. Ellison, Tent Revivalist

Acknowledgements

I am forever grateful for the love, support and unwavering faith shown to me by Neely Krispin, and Kaidyn Hughes, that kept me pressing on to bring Cal to life. A deep debt of gratitude is owed for the patience and skill of editor and author Elizabeth Lyon. I also give great thanks to Rev. Kay Hunter who mentored me and introduced me to my spiritual path. And most of all to my grandmother, Ruth Simmons, whose steady faith and endless unconditional love are the compass I aspire to follow every day.

FICTION

Historical fiction that lives

The Bookseller's Sonnets

Andi Rosenthal

The Bookseller's Sonnets intertwines three love stories with a tale of religious identity and mystery spanning five hundred years and three countries.

Paperback: 978-1-84694-342-3 ebook: 978-184694-626-4

Birds of the Nile

An Egyptian Adventure

N.E. David

Ex-diplomat Michael Blake wanted a quiet birding trip up the Nile – he wasn't expecting a revolution.

Paperback: 978-1-78279-158-4 ebook: 978-1-78279-157-7

Blood Profit$

The Lithium Conspiracy

J. Victor Tomaszek, James N. Patrick, Sr.

The blood of the many for the profits of the few... *Blood Profit$* will take you into the cigar-smoke-filled room where American policy and laws are really made.

Paperback: 978-1-78279-483-7 ebook: 978-1-78279-277-2

The Burden

A Family Saga

N.E. David

Frank will do anything to keep his mother and father apart. But he's carrying baggage – and it might just weigh him down ...

Paperback: 978-1-78279-936-8 ebook: 978-1-78279-937-5

The Cause
Roderick Vincent
The second American Revolution will be a fire lit from
an internal spark.
Paperback: 978-1-78279-763-0 ebook: 978-1-78279-762-3

Don't Drink and Fly
The Story of Bernice O'Hanlon: Part One
Cathie Devitt
Bernice is a witch living in Glasgow. She loses her way in her
life and wanders off the beaten track looking for the garden of
enlightenment.
Paperback: 978-1-78279-016-7 ebook: 978-1-78279-015-0

Gag
Melissa Unger
One rainy afternoon in a Brooklyn diner, Peter Howland
punctures an egg with his fork. Repulsed, Peter pushes the
plate away and never eats again.
Paperback: 978-1-78279-564-3 ebook: 978-1-78279-563-6

The Master Yeshua
The Undiscovered Gospel of Joseph
Joyce Luck
Jesus is not who you think he is. The year is 75 CE. Joseph
ben Jude is frail and ailing, but he has a prophecy to fulfi l ...
Paperback: 978-1-78279-974-0 ebook: 978-1-78279-975-7

On the Far Side, There's a Boy
Paula Coston
Martine Haslett, a thirty-something 1980s woman, plays hard
on the fringes of the London drag club scene until one night
which prompts her to sign up to a charity. She writes to a
young Sri Lankan boy, with consequences far and long.
Paperback: 978-1-78279-574-2 ebook: 978-1-78279-573-5

Tuareg
Alberto Vazquez-Figueroa
With over 5 million copies sold worldwide, *Tuareg* is a classic
adventure story from best-selling author Alberto Vazquez-
Figueroa, about honour, revenge and a clash of cultures.
Paperback: 978-1-84694-192-4

Readers of ebooks can buy or view any of these bestsellers by
clicking on the live link in the title. Most titles are published
in paperback and as an ebook. Paperbacks are available in
traditional bookshops. Both print and ebook formats are
available online.

Find more titles and sign up to our readers' newslett er at
http://www.johnhuntpublishing.com/fiction

Follow us on Facebook at https://www.facebook.com/
JHPfiction and Twitter at https://twitter.com/JHPFiction